Hope you like the book

Jeffrey Cross

Copyright © 2022 Jeffrey D. Crosby

All rights reserved. No part of this book may be reproduced in any fashion without express written permission of the publisher.

The characters and events portrayed in this book are fictitious. Any similarity to real persons, living or dead, is coincidental and not intended by the author.

Published by Jeffrey D. Crosby

P.O.Box 6704, Aurora, IL. 605989, USA

Jeffrey@jcrosby-books.com

ISBN: 978-1-7359387-5-2. Paperback

ISBN: 978-1-7359387-6-9 Ebook - epub

ISBN: 978-1-7359387-8-3. Ebook - mobi

ISBN: 978-1-7359387-7-6 Audio

Cover design: Vibrant Designs

Writing Coach: Jim Surowiecki

V0427

Table of Contents

Chapter 1 | Favor for Glenn 1
Chapter 2 | The Library 5
Chapter 3 | View from Afar 15
Chapter 4 | Talk with Old Friends 19
Chapter 5 | It's Not So Bad 25
Chapter 6 | Talk with Glenn 31
Chapter 7 | You Mean, Like Ghosts? 37
Chapter 8 | An Expert's Opinion 47
Chapter 9 | The New VIP 59
Chapter 10 | Wake-up Call 67
Chapter 11 | Act of Anger 71
Chapter 12 | Get Serious 77
Chapter 13 | Dead, Like Not Alive 83
Chapter 14 | Good Old Jackson 91
Chapter 15 | Chocolate is Fine 95
Chapter 16 | Attack from Mars 101
Chapter 17 | Time in the Chair 107
Chapter 18 | Puppet Master 111
Chapter 19 | I Don't Do Weird 117
Chapter 20 | Visit to a Graveyard 123
Chapter 21 | Just Enough Rope 131
Chapter 22 | Spilled Beans 141
Chapter 23 | You're Kidding Right? 149
Chapter 24 | Valuable Yes, Safe No 159
Chapter 25 | New Understanding 165
Chapter 26 | Trip to the Zoo 171
Chapter 27 | Please Henrietta 179
Chapter 28 | I Don't Want to Know 193
Chapter 29 | The Merry-Go-Round 201
Chapter 30 | Your Choice 211
Author's Note 217

Alternate Ending 219

Dedication

To My Mother
I love you and miss you.

Acknowledgments

Besides my wife, who supported me through every step, I wanted to name some other people whose support and advice helped bring this book to life.

Jim Surowiecki, Wendy & Todd Brown, Ranissa & Darnell Scott, Marcia Holt, Stephanie Brown, Mike and Mary Whitcomb, George Gecas and Jessica Mathias.

The following people allowed me to use their likeness when creating some of my characters. I have listed them in order of appearance in the book and I will leave it to them to tell you who was who.

George Gecas, Jim Surowiecki, Mike and Mary Whitcomb.

I also wanted to include a link to a company named in the story - www.naturalcollectivellc.com[1]

---

1. http://www.naturalcollectivellc.com

Chapter 1
Favor for Glenn

Quillon stared at the collection of pills in the little reminder box. "It's Tuesday, right?" he said toward the phone lying on the table.

"You're kidding?" came the reply.

"It's this new shift, Glenn. Working nights is really messing with me."

"Yes, it's Tuesday," said Glenn. "And if you remember, you requested the change."

"Darn, I missed a dose," said Quillon, staring at the pillbox. He clicked it closed and tossed it back on the table. "Well, nothing I can do about it now."

"I don't understand why you changed sites, anyway. That was a great site. Wondering around the mall, checking out the girls. Not much to look at in that warehouse overnight."

"Like I said, I was having trouble sleeping and decided that since I was up all night, why not get paid for it?"

"I only bring this up because I care about you, but you know your doctor wanted you to try being more social. That's why I got you posted at that mall. It's a primo site, and I took some heat for posting you there." When Quillon didn't answer, Glenn continued, "What's he going to say about you isolating yourself again?"

"Nothing, I don't plan on telling him. I just need some time to get the dreams back under control again." When there was no response from the phone, Quillon asked, "Glenn, are you there?"

"When did the dreams return?" asked Glenn trying his best to hide the concern in his voice.

"About a month now," said Quillon, leaning back on the couch, wishing he had not let the dream thing slip out.

"Is it like before? Is she telling you to hurt yourself again?"

"No, it's not like before. They don't last long. It's mostly about the times we spent together, before..."

There was a long pause, but both Glenn and Quillon knew the unspoken words.

"Have you told anyone?" asked Glenn finally. "Do you think you will have to go back into treatment?"

The worry in Glenn's voice was clear. Quillon shook his head and said, "I'm okay. They said I would have flashbacks as my memories returned. I promise, I'm okay to work." Quillon paused, then added, "I'll talk to someone if it gets worse."

"Good, then we can get back to the reason for my call?"

"You know I don't enjoy working those kinds of events," said Quillon. "Besides, I'm still getting used to the new hours and don't really want to come in on my day or night off, whichever it is."

"I really need your help," said Glenn, putting as much drama into his voice as he could without chuckling. He paused, then continued, "John called off again. It's just for six hours and you will get paid for eight. Besides, I'll have someone cover your next shift so you can get another day off."

Quillon stared at the phone, trying to think of a good reason to say no. He could hear the stress in his friend's voice. Glenn had always been there for him during his bad times. He had even gotten him this job. Quillon just wasn't in the mood to work a party.

"I really need your help on this," said Glenn, this time his voice was serious. "I'll make sure you get posted in a spot away from the main party."

Quillon let out his breath in a sigh.

When Glenn heard it, he understood the meaning. "Thanks Quill. You really saved my bacon."

"I haven't forgotten how much I owe you. Text me the information."

"You got it." There was a slight pause, then Glenn said, "One more thing, please wear a clean uniform."

"Funny," Quillon replied as he ended the call. He could hear the smile in Glenn's voice, but knew he had reason to say it. Quillon looked around at his apartment. Clothes scattered here and there. He picked up the pillbox, stared at it a few seconds, tossed it back on the table and said, "I'll deal with that later. Right now, I got to do something about the laundry."

Chapter 2
The Library

The ride to the Foundation was almost as much a mystery as the Foundation itself. He didn't have a car, so Glenn gave him and a few others a ride to the site in his panel van. He only caught a few glimpses of the outside, but mostly, what he saw were trees.

The inside of the Foundation offered a lot to see. The one thing he quickly learned was the Foundation had money. Lots and lots of money.

They got their briefing and were told not to speak to the guests unless spoken to. The party was going to be attended by some of the richest people in the world.

With that, Glenn left Quillon standing at a receptionist desk near the entrance. "Wait here. I got to get the others to their stations," said Glenn as he walked off.

Quillon felt awkward standing alone at the entrance. He could see the valets gathering and knew guests would arrive soon. He looked around. Not seeing Glenn, he mumbled, "If working the door is your idea of not dealing with guests, we're going to have a long talk."

"This way," said a dark suited man about thirty, as he walked past Quillon without stopping. Quillon just stared, not sure if the man was talking to him.

"Move it," said the man, as he adjusted his jacket, which Quillon knew by now, hid something.

Quillon followed the prompting of his new friend, and they quickly reached a corridor that met up with the lobby. It was wider than what he expected and long. The dark redwood paneling and recessed lighting, give it a somewhat modern look. A red and gold carpet extended its full length, which Quillon guessed was about forty feet. The only doorway was halfway down on the right.

At first Quillon thought the doorway led to another hallway, but discovered it was a double wide entrance to an impressive looking space, almost twice the size of his apartment, filled with books and display cases. He guessed it extended the full length of the hallway. While the hallway had a modern, almost executive look, this room was from a different time. It had a beautifully raised and tiled ceiling that had to be twelve feet high, if not higher. Suspended from the ceiling were several lights with ornamented green and red glass shades. The dark wood walls had carved, ornamented columns set into it about every ten feet. The floors, also of dark wood, had several large and beautiful Oriental rugs, each of which, he guessed, cost more than the car he was thinking about buying.

"Wow, what a great place," Quillon said, looking around. "If you added a pool table and a door, you'd really have something."

"This is the research library," said his escort. "The only reason you're here is because it doesn't have a door. You're to keep people out. Talk to them as little as possible, and touch nothing. Do you think you can do that?"

"You must be new," said Quillon, tapping his side, mimicking the man's behavior with his jacket. "You really need to stop touching your gun. People will notice."

The man adjusted his jacket again, gave Quillon a stern look and said, "Remember, no one gets in, and you do not leave until relieved!"

"This isn't my first job. I know the drill," said Quillon, looking around. "I guess if I have to go, I can find a nice, quiet corner."

Quillon could see that the man had no sense of humor. He touched the mic of the radio, strapped to the shoulder epaulet of his uniform, and quickly added, "Only kidding, I'll radio if I need anything."

The man gave the room one last look around, paused, then left, saying nothing else. Before the man left, Quillon thought he saw a strange look on the man's face. Quillon couldn't decide if that look was that of a person leaving a shrine, or a place of horror. Either way, Quillon was glad to be rid of him. Looking around, he decided to take a tour of his new domain.

Almost all the books were old, many of them with titles in foreign languages. A few of them were in display cases, opened to strange and sometimes unnerving illustrations. There were some with plants, others with strange colored wheels, and then there were the ones of people. Most showed what looked like rituals. In the more disturbing ones, people were being killed or eaten by horrible, unearthly, even demonic looking creatures.

Many of the cases contained odd items, including some elements of clothing, fragments of stones, and a few that looked like tools. One of them contained several knives, all different sizes and styles.

It took Quillon about thirty minutes to make his way around the library, and he was relieved to be back at the entrance. "I think I know now what that guy was thinking when he left," said Quillon in a low voice. He spoke out loud, more to give himself company than anything else.

Across from the entrance, against the wall, was a desk. He had almost missed it because it was so plain. *Well, I know where I'm going to spend the rest of the night,* he thought. That's when he noticed a small glass case on the credenza behind the desk.

"If that has a head in it, I'm out of here," he mumbled as he walked over to it. To his surprise, and relief, it only contained a highly decorated box. It was about a foot long. Its width and height were both about eight inches.

As he studied the box, it reminded him of some of the Japanese puzzle boxes he had collected when he was younger. He had gotten good at them and had a decent collection before the accident.

"You'll find the gift shop is in the main lobby," came a voice behind him. Turning, Quillon saw a thin older man dressed in a tuxedo standing in the doorway. Quillon could not place his age, somewhere between mid 50s and early 60s. He was a little shorter than Quillon, had short white hair, and a close-cut beard. He carried himself with a sense of authority, which was softened by a slight smile.

Quillon had been told that he would not have to deal with anyone at this post, and it took a few seconds to remember why he was here. He regained his composure and took a few steps toward the man, put his best official face on, and with his right hand slightly outstretched before him said, "Sorry, but this room is not open for visitors."

"I was about to tell you the same thing," said the man as he casually walked past Quillon toward the desk.

"I'm supposed to be here," said Quillon. "I'm with security for the party."

"So I guessed," said the man as he switched on a lamp on the desk. "The uniform gave it away."

During Quillon's short time in security, he never really dealt with any problem people. Most of the people he talked to politely responded to his instruction without questions. He was not sure how best to handle this situation. He thought back to some of his training videos. Almost without thinking, he said, "I'm sorry, sir, but this room is closed. If you don't leave, you will force me to call someone."

"My name is Professor Ian Georges. I'm a regent of this foundation. In fact, that party out there is in my honor. I just released a new book on the study of Haiku from the 15th to 19th century." Georges paused, studied Quillon, and decided that he had no idea what he was talking about. "I got bored and wanted to get away. This is our research library, and I want to spend a little time here. So, if you don't mind," said Georges, pointing to the door.

"I can't leave," said Quillon, startled at the man's request. "I'll get in trouble."

"I'll cover for you with your boss. You can go home for all I care. Tell me your name."

"Quillon."

There was a brief pause, followed by a laugh that took Quillon by surprise. He worried the Professor was going to turn into one of those problem drunks. He was relieved when the laughter ended in a smile.

"Quillon, that's quite a coincidence," said Georges, still smiling.

"I don't understand," said Quillon, still not sure how to handle the smiling man.

"Tell me, Quillon, why were you looking at that box?"

"It reminds me of a puzzle box," said Quillon, glancing back at the box. "They were a hobby of mine for a while when I was younger."

"You're correct, Quillon. It is very special. One of a kind. Only a handful of people have seen it."

Georges' repeated use of his name was bothering Quillon.

"It looks like some of the Japanese ones I had, but I can't figure out what style it is. My guess would be a maze or sliding."

"You know your puzzle boxes, Quillon. I'm a fan of many of Japan's finer arts. My passion is the Haiku. Like you, I'm also a fan of puzzle boxes. I have in my collection what many believed to be one of the oldest known working puzzle boxes. It's from 1800s and comes from the Hakone region. This one is much older than that. In fact, we do not know how old it is, or how it works. It doesn't appear to be wood, and the symbols and patterns do not match any I recognize."

"Why do you keep repeating my name? Do you think it's funny or something?"

"No Quillon, nothing like that," Georges, his hand slightly pointing toward the box. "I just think it's amusing that someone named Quillon would be attracted to a Quillon dagger."

"What dagger?" asked Quillon, as he adjusted the volume of the radio clipped to his belt to make sure it was on.

"That's the interesting part, Quillon. We never figured out how to open the box, but thanks to modern technology, we peeked inside. Guess what we found?"

"A dagger," said Quillon, relieved he was following where the Professor was leading with his tale. He let his hand drop from the radio to his side.

"Not just any dagger, a Quillon dagger. We can't date the box, but we can date the dagger."

"That's interesting, but I think I'm going to take your first suggestion and leave," said Quillon. He wasn't sure where he was going to spend the rest of the shift, but he didn't want to spend it listening to a lecture.

"That's fine, but before you leave, why don't you try opening the box?"

Quillon looked back at the box in the display case. He hadn't messed with puzzle boxes since his sister had died. Back then, he just couldn't find the energy to focus his mind on things for a long time. He walked back to the display case and studied the box.

"So, just how good are you with puzzle boxes?" asked Georges, as he stepped over to the display case and stood beside Quillon.

Quillon hadn't heard the man approach and was a little startled. He looked back at the box and after a few seconds said, "Before I quit, I had a few level 10 boxes."

"That's impressive," said Georges. "I don't know how we would rate this one, but if you opened it, you would probably be the first since the 14th century."

"How do you know that?"

"I told you we think the box contains a Quillon dagger. Those were very popular in the 14th century. The truth is, the box was lost for some time. Once our Foundation acquired it, the box sat forgotten in our archives until I rediscovered it about 25 years ago. So, I can't really tell you the last time it was opened. I can tell you I have tried several times and could not open it."

"Why don't you just hire someone? I'm sure there are lots of people out there that would like to give it a shot."

"That's not how we do things here. They put it away for a reason, and the Foundation would prefer that the knowledge of its existence remains limited."

Quillon looked around. He now saw the collection of locked displays and case differently. "So, you guys are collectors?"

Georges looked around and smiled. "We do possess a lot of old, unique, and valuable items. Sometimes I forget that."

"Okay," said Quillon, "I will try it, but don't blame me if I break it. Something that old might be brittle."

"You will find this in great shape," said Georges, as he used a swipe key to unlock the case.

Quillon hesitated when Georges offered him the box. "Don't I need to put on gloves?"

"I'm all out," said Georges with a smile. "Like I said, it's in good shape. Go ahead, take it."

The box was not as heavy as he imagined. Especially for one that supposedly had a dagger inside. It also had a strange feel to it. Almost like it was slippery. He held it up to the light and studied the sides for any evidence of a line caused by sliding pieces. After that, he put a little pressure on each edge, looking to see if any of the sides or top had any play in them.

"I don't see any obvious joints," said Quillon. "Now, I'm going to check for pressure points." While he was slowly using his finger to follow the design of the flowing symbols, he thought he felt a raised point. He held it up to the light and studied the surface. He saw a section of design that appeared slightly higher than the others, almost like a slight bulge or warp. "I think I found something," he said as he checked the other sides for something similar.

"Really?" said Georges, "So soon? I've spent years studying this thing."

"I haven't opened it yet, but I have heard of boxes that have pressure points that need to be pressed in order to allow other smaller internal pieces to move. They fall by gravity once the lock is released, making room for other pieces to slide. I've never seen one."

Quillon held down the pressure point, put the box close to his ear as he rocked the box back and forth, hoping to hear something sliding. "No good. I heard something moving, but I think it is the knife."

"Well, you got further than me," said Georges with his hand out for the box.

"I'm not done yet. If it's, okay?"

Georges used his hand to signal his approval.

Quillon held down the pressure point and studied the surfaces again. He saw the slight suggestion of another raised point. "Found you," he said. With two pressure points, one on each side of the box, he checked for evidence of sliding pieces. He found, instead, what looked like another pressure point. He guessed that there was an order in which the points had to be pressed for another one to be revealed, almost like a combination.

It took him several tries until he was holding down pressure points on fives sides; the box held with the fingers of both hands. When he saw a pressure point on what he considered the top side, he adjusted his grip, so all pressure points were pressed, and used his free finger to press the new pressure point. To his surprise, it seemed to allow him to press the surface deeper than any of the other. "I hope this is the last point. I am running out of fingers." He pressed hard. A tingle of excitement grew in his stomach as he felt the spot he was pressing sink into the surface. That tingle vanished, replaced by confusion, as he felt a sharp pain. A pain which caused him to drop the box. Looking at his finger, he saw blood. "Ouch," he said, and put his finger in his mouth.

"I wouldn't do that," said a man's voice from the direction of the doorway.

Both Quillon and Georges turned almost in unison. Quillon relaxed slightly when he saw a thin young man with dark hair dressed in a tuxedo. *Another lost party goer,* he thought.

The man walked casually towards Quillon and Georges, a slight smile on his face, as if they were old friends. "I have read stories where some societies used poison on needles to kill the person who opened their puzzle boxes."

"Poison?" said Quillon, looking at his finger.

"Strange custom," said the man as he continued his advance. "They would train people, special people, whose job it was to open the box, as you just did. These people accepted this role, knowing when they did, they would die."

"This area is not open to the public," said Georges. "If you return to the lobby, I will see that you get a signed copy of my book."

"I'm looking for something more valuable than that, and thanks to your guard, I have found it."

Quillon followed the man's eyes, and saw the box lying on the ground with its contents, a six inch shining dagger with blood red wrapping around the hilt, on the ground a few inches away. Quillon reached for the dagger at the same time as the man, but got there first. It felt cold and gave him a shock like a when you press your tongue against a battery. He dropped it, and when he reached for it again, he found it in the stranger's hand.

Chapter 3
View from Afar

Quillon remembered the blade, and the sharp pain as it entered his chest. What happened next wasn't clear. He was sure he must have been dreaming, but it was almost like he was watching someone else's dream. A disturbing dream full of sights and smells he could not relate to. Even more disturbing was the cold and the darkness. He could almost feel both pressing in on him. The world around him made little sense. The sky churned with a mixture of dark and grey, briefly illuminated with streaks of red and yellow. He could not distinguish where the sky ended and the ground began. An occasional dark point that reached upward at a strange angle marked the landscape. They almost seem to change shape each time the sky flashed.

He saw trails of movement ahead of him in what looked like a combination of low grasses and fog. At times, it looked like water moving. Strange dark churning water. At other times, it reminded him of the graveyard fog he had seen in one of those old scary monster movies he watched as a kid.

Quillon watched the movement, some distant, and others uncomfortably near, surprised that he did not feel fear. What he felt was a strange tingling in what he guessed were his fingertips, followed by an icy chill each time he saw the grasses move. He watched one of these nearby trails as it moved to his left and towards the area behind him. Turning, he saw what looked like a dark tunnel floating in the air. A feeling of excitement mixed with hunger came over him as he stared into the tunnel. He felt himself drawn to the small opening.

At the end of the dark tunnel, he could see people in a room that looked familiar. It was almost like he was watching it on television. The colors were strange and there was no sound. He struggled to understand what he was seeing. There inside that little room was a sight that made the mad world behind him seem welcoming.

Lying on the floor of that little room was a body. One that Quillon was sure belonged to him. It was wearing his uniform, complete with a blood-soaked stain on its chest.

Quillon made a mental note to add this dream to his journal so he could talk about it at his next session. Studying the scene, he noticed a strange glow coming from the body's chest. Seeing that, he could almost feel the pain of the blade again. The pain was real and with it came a feeling of panic, as he realized it was his body lying there.

There was another sharp jab of pain, soon followed by another. This time, he noticed that with each jab of pain, the little window appeared to get wider. The glow from his body also increased. It was then he noticed an object on the floor beside him echoed the glow from his body. It was the dagger. The one he had struggled over.

Now, once again, he saw a hand grab it. Following the arm brought him to the face of the man that had stabbed him. The man stood over Quillon, dagger in hand, once more. It was then Quillon saw the dagger was not pointing at the body on the floor. Both the blade and the man's stare were fixed on something deep inside the dark tunnel.

Quillon had a momentary feeling of fear when he realized the man was staring at him. Anger quickly replaced that fear, so strong it surprised him. Quillon felt the urge to reach out and crush the man. A strong, almost overpowering feeling of hunger followed.

Quillon pressed against the dark window and felt more anger as he realized it was too small for him to get through. Quillon returned his attention to the man and saw him standing, still as death, his eyes locked on Quillon's. Eyes that showed both surprise and terror. The man looked at the dagger in his hand and back to the body on the ground. It was then that another figure stepped into view. One that upset Quillon more than seeing his body on the ground.

Standing next to Quillon's body was the figure of a small child, only five years of age. She was wearing a white dress that matched the paleness of her skin. It was his little sister, Henrietta. Quillon was afraid this dream had become another of those painful nightmares from his past. Dreams he had worked so hard to put back into the past where they belonged. But, here she was again, in her little white dress, looking just like she did the last time he saw her, laying in the small white coffin they buried her in.

Quillon prepared himself for what he feared could come next. She would blame him again, not in so many words, but more in the way she would stare, beckoning him to follow her to the grave.

He steadied his mind for her gaze, surprised when she knelt and placed her small hand over the glow on his chest. As he watched, the glow lessen. As it did, there was a horrible burning sensation, followed by a strange feeling of anger, almost hate. The room spun, and he soon had the feeling he was falling.

Quillon felt the muscles in his body shake uncontrollably. When it stopped, he was afraid to do anything. He slowly opened his eyes, blinking a few times at the brightness, and took a deep breath as the sounds of the room and the pain from the wound in his chest poured back into his mind. The pain was worse than anything he had felt in his dream. He struggled for each breath, almost wishing he could return to his dream.

Quillon fought through the pain and discovered his sister and his attacker were gone, replaced by the figure of Professor Georges. He heard the professor's voice, but could not focus enough to understand him. He felt someone grab his feet and saw the room move. It took him a few seconds to understand that someone had dragged him from the library.

People asking him questions soon surrounded Quillon. He felt himself being moved to a stretcher and lifted into the air.

Quillon looked to the left and saw the Professor following along, not looking at him, but giving instruction to others who joined him. Quillon looked to his right, and just before he passed out, he saw Henrietta.

Chapter 4
Talk with Old Friends

Georges stared into the wall safe, as if waiting for the puzzle box that held the dagger to move on its own. They had been retrieved from the thief as he attempted to escape. The wall safe of his office seemed like the best place to keep it for now. He knew he would have trouble explaining why forbidden magic like this was in the research library and not locked away, out of reach, in the upper floor vaults where it belonged.

Being the Grand Master of the Golden Mean Foundation let him stretch the rules a bit. After all, he and his predecessors had created most of them. Still, he expected to get some grief from the other regents on the upcoming video conference call. Thankfully, the large monitor on the wall across from his desk was empty. He knew soon it would be full of the grim faces of his fellow regents, many of which were eagerly awaiting their chance at his chair.

Inside the safe, next to the box, was a bottle of Glenlivet single malt scotch whisky. A little something he needed when preparing for these video chats. The bottle showed that these meetings had not been that frequent, a small blessing at least.

As Georges reached for the bottle, his hand paused inches away. Then, as if he was reaching into the mouth of a lion, he quickly grabbed the bottle from the safe.

Georges studied the box again, then slowly closed the safe door. He breathed a sigh as he heard the movements of the latch securing the safe door. Looking at the bottle in his hand, Georges could barely see the shaking that had been so obvious earlier. Still, he was going to find the bottle a less disturbing resting space.

Several overlapping beeps from the monitor behind him alerted Georges that the other regents had joined, so their conference could now begin. He looked at the bottle in his hand, wishing that he had acted a few minutes sooner. He wondered if he should just pour that drink and deal with the criticism that would soon follow. Georges had a history and there were rivals in the faces waiting on the screen that would use that against him.

Georges looked back at the door of the wall safe, then thought back to what he had just experienced. A slight smile came to his lips as he reached for a glass and poured himself two fingers' worth. He knew he was more afraid of what had just happened than the criticism of these know-it-alls.

"Sir, we are waiting!"

It was the voice of Jordan Elliott. Georges knew Elliott would be the first to speak. The formality in the voice failed to hide the disdain Elliott felt for Georges. It was a rare meeting, when Elliott did not make some comment about Georges' rights to the position of Grand Master.

Georges turned to see a collection of twelve faces on the large monitor, most with fake office walls or windows in the background. Georges smiled at one face, who was clearly sitting on a real lounge chair, with real palm trees and a large white and red roof building in the background. The area behind him was busy with people dressed in bathing suits of varying degrees of modesty. It was Yuri Lebedev, the only regent he could call a friend. Seeing Yuri, with his aviator sunglasses perched on a cream covered nose and white ear buds sticking out like antennas, almost made the meeting worthwhile.

"My apologies, Yuri, for interrupting your vacation, but it is an emergency," said Georges, as he placed his glass on the desk in front of him and sat down. He no longer cared if the glass was in plain view. In fact, he hoped Elliott would launch into one of his discussions on his family lineage. It would give him a chance to hand this whole mess off to someone else.

Georges took a few seconds to adjust his chair, knowing the delay would irritate Elliott. He closed the screen of the laptop on his desk, focused on the group of faces, and said slowly and clearly, "There has been a summoning. Forbidden magic was used." Georges paused, then said, "The Necro Box."

When Georges did not hear a reply, he studied the faces, and realized that, because of his position, he was the only one that had a true understanding of what he was referring to. He knew he would need to explain the threat and, unfortunately, why he had possession of it.

"Why would you allow the use of forbidden magic?" asked Elliott. "Everyone knows that requires the approval of all the Foundation chairs, and I would have never approved something as dangerous as that. I think it's clear to everyone here that you have overstepped your privileges as Grand Master this time."

Georges could see the others look away. It was clear none of them wanted to endure another of these discussions on authority. "This has nothing to do with titles, Elliott! I told you this was an emergency. I did not sanction it. It was an accident started by outsiders."

"Enough!" said Yuri. "We have more important things to worry about. Grand Master, I think we are going to need a little more information on this forbidden magic to understand this emergency."

Georges was thankful for Yuri's intervention, but wondered if he would have his support once he fully explained things. He looked from face to face, thinking about where best to start. "I think it's best if I show you," he said as he retrieved the box from his safe and placed it on the desk in front of him. He moved it until everyone said they had a good view of it.

"I think I've seen this Necro Box before," said a man, maybe ten years Georges' senior. "In fact, I think it was your grandfather that showed it to me."

"That's correct Regent Wickmayer," said Georges. "It's from the Surowiecki Collection, acquired by my grandfather when he was Grand Master."

"And it's this box that contains this forbidden magic?" asked Regent Wickmayer.

"I have spent the last twenty-five years researching the Necro Box. It was acquired from the estate of a man named Surowiecki, along with a collection of ancient documents. The few that I have been able to translate tell the story of a group of mages who stole and used forbidden magic that released an undesirable evil, they referred to as the *Madness*. This box, which they called the Necro Box, contains a summoning dagger. Because the dagger and the box are named along with the stolen magic, the Foundation labeled it as forbidden as well."

"I'm confused," said a younger regent name Ashwind, his voice showing his irritation. "You called us here for an emergency meeting. You said forbidden magic was used. Are you saying this 'Madness' has been summoned again?"

Georges took a sip, then said, "The Necro Box was opened, and the summoning dagger was used. A portal was created that contained something. I'm not sure what's within it."

"How was this allowed to happen?" asked another Regent.

Georges was not sure who asked the question because he was putting the box back into the safe. As he returned to his seat, he said, "The Necro Box was in the research library, so I could do some studies based on new information I discovered in the Surowiecki papers. I left the party early to continue my work and discovered Quillon, a security guard from the company we hired for the party, was on duty there. The young man was a puzzle fan. After talking for a while, I asked him to try his hand at opening the Necro Box. God knows I've had no luck. While he was working on it, an unknown person entered and attempted to steal it. Somehow, in the middle of the theft, the box opened, and the dagger fell out. Quillon and the thief struggled over the dagger and Quillon was stabbed. That summoned a portal."

"You must have misspoken, Grand Master," said Elliott, looking at Georges' glass. "I think you meant Summoning Circle instead of Portal."

Georges took another sip and said, "I'm not as experienced as you in summoning, but I know the difference between a portal and a circle." Georges could feel his temper rising and did his best to control it as he continued. "I can guarantee you there is a portal floating in the research library right now."

There was silence for several minutes until Yuri spoke. "You said the summoning opened a portal, but nothing crossed over? What have you done to contain the situation?"

"The only witnesses to the event are myself, Quillon, and the thief," said Georges, fingering the edge of his glass, wishing he had time to refill it. He took a breath and continued, "The thief is being detained in one of our special rooms. We transported Quillon to our hospital. I will check on him after this meeting. I'm sure we will work out something with him. If not, we have other less desirable ways to control this."

"And the portal?" asked Yuri.

Georges paused for a few seconds. He knew what he needed to do next but dreaded doing it. He touched the rim of the empty glass on his desk, then said, "As you know, my area of expertise is in historical documents. I'm a researcher. Actual summoning and protection spells are an area we all recognize as Regent Elliot's expertise. As a result, I'm asking for his guidance."

"I accept that invitation," said Elliot. Then, with only a momentary paused he continued, "My team and I will be there tomorrow. I'm sure we will be able to quickly neutralize this situation."

"Why do you think it is still open?" The question was out before Georges realized he said it. George pushed the glass away. It was bad enough that he would need to work with the man, but now he had given Elliott the opportunity to point out his ignorance on the subject.

"Without more information, I believe it results from a failure in the summoning process," said Elliott. "Do you have any ideas, Grand Master?"

The question surprised Georges. He had been expecting Elliott to break into a long lecture. He made use of the pause before he answered to make it look like he was deep in honest thought. Finally, he responded with, "I have no idea."

"In that case," said Elliott. "I'll need access to all the information you have on the items used during the summoning."

"I have not translated all the documents, but I'll make available what I have," said Georges.

"I'm sure you have taken reasonable actions to deal with the threat," said Elliott. "However, I will speak with my people after this meeting ends. We will come up with a list of the proper protection needed to help control it."

Georges forced a smile and said, "I look forward to your visit. However, I would caution anyone else from visiting until we have a better understanding of the danger we are facing. In fact, I would ask that we postpone our upcoming annual meeting next week."

There was a pause, followed by the voice of Regent Wickmayer. "Grand Master, I understand your concerns, but if you take more than a week to resolve this, I think it would be best if we all apply our expertise."

"Then I'll see you all next week. With that, I think it is time to close this meeting." Georges clicked off the conference and sat staring at the empty screen. He fingered the rim of the empty glass before him, then mumbled, "One more, before I decide how to deal with our witnesses."

Chapter 5
It's Not So Bad

The steady beeping of the monitor was the first thing to tell Quillon that something was wrong. He tried to open his eyes, but the brightness forced him to close them again. His mouth was dry, and he could almost taste each breath he was taking. He felt strange. Not sure if he was awake or not.

Suddenly, the images from the dream poured back into his mind. The blade, the blood, the horrible pain in his chest. These were quickly replaced by the most disturbing image of Henrietta standing over him.

Quillon opened his eyes, glanced around, fearing what he would see. At first, he was relieved to find he was in what looked like a hospital room. That relief vanished when the sounds of the monitor and the tubes in his arm confirmed he was in fact in a hospital room.

He opened his mouth to speak, but not much more than a groan came out. It was enough to get the attention of the two individuals that were talking nearby.

"Mr. Thomas. My name is Doctor Demetrio. You can call me Doctor D if you like. I just wanted to see if you know where you are?"

Quillon turned his head and tried to rise, but found he could not move.

"You are in a private hospital. Please do not move. We don't want you to injure yourself again. You are also on medications that may make you sleepy. If you understand what I'm saying, please nod and I will explain your condition."

"Sleepy," said Quillon, attempting to nod his understanding.

"What do you remember, Mr. Thomas?" When Quillon did not answer, Doctor Demetrio said, "Please concentrate, Mr. Thomas."

"Bad dream. Henrietta," mumbled Quillon.

Quillon felt so sleepy. He feared falling back into that dream and weakly shook his head no in protest and said, "Please Henrietta, I'm sorry."

"Do you remember being attacked, Mr. Thomas? Do you remember being stabbed?"

Quillon remembered something about a dagger, but those images were quickly mixed with others that made little sense. "Yes, the dagger," said Quillon in almost a whisper. The dryness of his lips prevented him from saying more.

"We are going to give you some ice, Mr. Thomas. Suck on it, but don't swallow it."

The coldness of the ice in his mouth gave him something real to focus on. Up to this point, he still wasn't sure if he was dreaming. He looked around again at his surroundings. His head hurt, and he felt an ache in his chest. It started as a tingle but grew to be more painful as he looked at the bandage on his chest. "What happened to me?" he said, still looking at his chest.

"You were stabbed," said Georges, who had been standing quietly listening, deciding if he would get involved. He stepped closer to Quillon, then continued. "You were helping me with a puzzle box. Do you remember?"

"I remember you," said Quillon as the jumble of images in his mind cleared. What it left was the puzzle box and the blade. "That guy tried to steal your knife." Quillon paused for a second, then in a voice that was louder and more excited than he had been using, said, "He stabbed me!" Quillon looked at his chest and said again, "That bastard stabbed me!"

"Calm down, Mr. Thomas," said Doctor Demetrio as he stepped forward and placed his hand on Quillon's shoulder. "It's not as bad as it looks. In fact, you were quite lucky. The blade did not reach any vital organs."

"But he stabbed me," repeated Quillon, not sure what wasn't vital. "Where is he? Did someone get him?"

"His name is Hugo Thornton, and yes, he is in custody. He will be dealt with properly," said Georges as calmly as he could. "We were also able to recover the items he tried to take. You have our thanks."

Quillon relaxed a little and looked back at his bandaged chest. It surprised him that the next thing that came into his mind was how long was he going to be out of work. Quillon had bills to pay. He had never paid attention to all that insurance stuff that they threw at him each year. Long term, short term, all he knew was he needed to talk to Glenn as soon as possible.

"You said it's not bad. How long am I going to need to be here? I need to let my boss and my landlord know what is going on."

"The Foundation will cover all your hospital expenses. We have also been in touch with your work." Georges smiled and continued, "It's the least we can do to show our thanks."

They are probably worried about getting sued, thought Quillon. He put that thought aside for now and said, "Thank you."

"You were fortunate," said Demetrio. "Your wounds should heal quickly. There was a little foreign matter that we could not remove. They are tiny and should not cause you any long-term issues."

"Foreign matter," said both Quillon and Georges at the same time.

"Minor really," said Demetrio. "Some splinters, or possibly the tip, came off the blade when it struck two of his ribs. We tried to remove them but had to stop because they seemed to work themselves deeper and we were having trouble with bleeding. We will do an evaluation again, but my team believes the pieces are small enough to not present any real complication." the doctor paused, then said, "You might set off a few metal detectors if you travel."

Quillon and Georges looked at the doctor. Both had an expression of concern on their faces. Both, for very different reasons.

Georges was the first to speak. "You left the pieces in?"

"I have seen other cases like this that had little to no complications later," said Demetrio. "Our chief concern is if they contained anything that might cause a reaction. I understand the blade was ancient. There is always the possibility of rust, or even bacteria, on something that old."

"Rust and bacteria," said Quillon, looking at his chest.

"It is a tiny chance, but it is something we are monitoring," said Demetrio. "Better safe than sorry."

"I can guarantee you won't find any decay," said Georges.

Quillon notice the Professor looked at him differently. In a manner that almost looked like he was afraid. Without taking his eyes off Quillon, Georges said, "Thank you, Doctor. Now, I need to spend some time alone with Mr. Thomas, if you don't mind."

Quillon had watched the discussion between Georges and the doctor. The way the doctor and his staff reacted to him made Quillon think the Professor might be more than the pleasant smiling person he remembered from the library.

Georges stood watching Quillon for several minutes after the doctor left the room. The silence made Quillon nervous. Not sure what to say, he decided the best thing to do was to thank him again for handling the hospital expenses.

Georges smiled and said, "This hospital is funded by my Foundation. I'm sure they are happy to have an interesting case to work on. What I'm curious about is what you're going to do once you check out."

"I thought you said you spoke to my work."

"We did," said Georges, pulling up a nearby chair. "They know we will handle your hospital stay. We also assured them we will not sue them for the poor job they did on protecting us."

Quillon stared at the professor. His brief relief over his financial woes crumbled. He stared up at the roof and let out a sigh.

"I have a great opportunity for you. One that would, I think, address any money concerns."

"Opportunity?" said Quillon, looking back at the Professor.

Georges leaned forward, and in a low voice, one Quillon understood was meant for only the two of them, said, "You may not know it, but you did something remarkable when you opened that box. What I need you to do is...," Georges looked around, then continued, "close it again."

"What?" said Quillon.

"It's a little embarrassing, but we can't seem to get the box to stay closed. I figured that since you opened it, you could close it, and we'll pay you a lot of money to try."

Chapter 6
Talk with Glenn

The burning and itching were becoming more and more difficult for Quillon to tolerate. It was coming from under the bandage that covered his chest. He could just see the edges of what he had been told was a rash extending beyond the bandages. He had complained about it all morning to his nurse, who had put an ointment on it each time. That helped, but only for a few hours. It would always come back, each time preceded by muscle spasms in his chest and a feeling of dizziness.

When the spasms came this time, he was in the middle of a conversation with Glenn. The pain stopped him in mid-sentence, and he almost dropped the phone. It took him several minutes before he could respond to Glenn's desperate questions about what was happening.

"It's this burning and itching," Quillon said. "It just doesn't stop."

"I had a friend that broke his leg," said Glenn sympathetically. "He said the itching was terrible. When they took his cast off, his skin was all white and peeling. He said it still itched for a few days."

"I've heard that story too, but this is different," said Quillon, looking at the dark red lines peeking out from under the bandages. "They say it is a rash, but I don't think so. I've seen it when they change the bandage, and it looks really strange."

"What do you mean, strange?"

"I've had a rash before," said Quillon, looking at the area around his bandage, "and this doesn't look like that. It has a pattern to it. Like lots of thin red lines. Kind of like what I imagine varicose veins would look like. It's all over my chest and keeps getting bigger. The lines are darker and thicker around the wound, and they spread outward like a spider web."

"And that's what made you scream?" asked Glenn.

"No, it's the spasms. I get these sharp pains in my chest, where I was stabbed, followed by muscle spasms. I tell people about it, but they just keep saying that's to be expected."

"Well, I don't know anyone who has been stabbed, except you, so they could be right," said Glenn.

"I know," said Quillon. "But it doesn't make it any easier to handle."

The pains came again. Quillon arched his back, then turned to one side, placing his arm that was in a sling across his chest and holding it against the chest with the other. He let the phone drop to his bed, more worried about the pain than continuing his talk.

When the pain didn't stop, he reached for the call button, but before he could use it, Doctor Demetrio entered.

"Looks like I got here right on time," said Demetrio, pressing the call button himself. He did his best to comfort Quillon until the pain passed. "Looks like you're still having spasms," said Demetrio, glancing at Quillon's chart.

"It's getting worse Doctor D." Calling the doctor by that name was strange, but he insisted so Quillon finally gave in.

"And the rash?" asked Demetrio.

"The worse the spasms get, the worse the rash gets. The ointment is less and less effective. It only lasts for a while." Quillon lifted his shirt and said, "Plus, I think it is getting bigger."

Doctor Demetrio looked at the rash and said, "It's normal to get redness around the area of a wound. I'm sure that both the redness and itching should go away in a few days. The muscle spasms might take longer. There was some muscle damage and possibly even some nerve damage. We will learn more once you start physical therapy."

"Are you sure this rash is normal? It's spreading."

"Our tests did not detect any toxins or evidence of infection. I will have our Dermatologist look at it. I'm sure he will want some pictures. We can prescribe something a little stronger for the rash and the spasm. Any other issues?"

"I have been having strange nightmares. Well, not really nightmares because they have happened in the daytime as well. They are full of strange sights and smells. Plus, I keep ending up back in the library where I was attacked. The worst part is the feeling just before and after the dreams that I'm being watched. The last one was horrible. My rash on my chest ached so bad, it woke me out of the dream."

"You have been through a traumatic experience. I'm not surprised. Many people who survive attacks experience something very much like the post-traumatic shock syndrome of veterans. If you like, I can give you something to help you sleep. I will refer you for physical therapy to help with the wound. I can also refer you to someone about your dreams."

"I have someone," said Quillon. "I was trying to keep that part of my life in the past."

"Well, in that case, I think we should be able to release you today, right after your blood transfusion," said Demetrio.

"Blood transfusion. Why do I need that?"

"You're a little anemic," said Demetrio. "It happens with injuries that result in blood loss. Normally, your body can replenish blood in a few days. Yours is lagging a bit. We're sure it's not the result of any internal bleeding, so it might have something to do with the foreign matter left inside. X-rays show that most of it has attached itself to a few of your rib bones."

"Is that also normal?"

"We are looking into it. The good thing is that it reduces the chance of the large pieces moving closer to a vital organ or getting into your bloodstream."

"But I'm okay, right?" asked Quillon.

"We wouldn't be releasing you if we thought it was a problem," said Demetrio with a smile. "You will need to come back in a few weeks for follow-ups. You can always come back early if you have any concerns, or if the pains or rash are still a problem."

Quillon thanked the doctor, and as he adjusted the sheets of his bed, he discovered his phone. He hesitated a few seconds, put the phone to his ear, said, "I guess you heard that?"

"About the dreams? Didn't hear a thing."

"Funny," said Quillon.

"I hope you are going to talk to someone about them," said Glenn. "Don't put it off like last time."

"This isn't like last time. These are different," said Quillon nervously. "I need to be careful. I don't want people to think that I have slipped. I'm not going back to that old life."

"You heard the doctor. PTSD is a real thing," said Glenn sternly. "People will understand it this time."

"I'm tired of having people poking around in my head," said Quillon, with a hint of anger. "You know I've learned a lot from my sessions. I can get things back under control. Besides, do you think that the Foundation will have anything to do with me if they think I'm crazy?"

"Crazy or not, if your doctor makes a note in your record, you're not coming back to work without getting evaluated. That much you should know by now."

"You going to turn me in?" asked Quillon, a little sharper than he wanted.

"I won't have to, but I'm also not going to let you drop it. That's what friends do."

"Thanks friend," said Quillon as he hung up. He slammed the phone down on the little table next to the bed, harder than he intended. He picked it up and was glad to see there were not any new cracks on the screen. Staring at it, he felt embarrassed. He knew Glenn was right. He was a friend and really the only one that had stuck with him during the bad time. Still, he feared going back to the way it was. "No, I'm going to handle this on my own," he said in a low voice, one that lacked the confidence he was looking for.

Chapter 7
You Mean, Like Ghosts?

Quillon pushed the multicolored mush on his plate around a few times. With each push of the plastic spork, there was a slight pain. *Succotash, what kind of name is that for food?* he thought. *Another good reason to get out of this place.*

Movement near the nurse's station in the hallway caught his attention. It was Doctor D. He saw the doctor study a chart the nurse handed him. *Good,* thought Quillon. *No more excuses. I'm done. I'm going to tell him I want to go home.*

As he watched the doctor, it surprised him to see him joined by Professor Georges. He could not hear what they were saying, but it was clear the doctor was concerned about something. He glanced in Quillon's direction several times.

Georges put his hand on the doctor's shoulder, took the chart from him, and looked at Quillon. Doctor D said something else, then, to Quillon's surprise, walked away.

What now? thought Quillon as he watched Georges flip through the pages of the chart. *He must know I can see him.*

A few seconds later, Georges gave Quillon a smile and headed toward the room.

"So, don't tell me you're also a doctor," said Quillon light heartedly.

Georges glanced at the chart in his hand and said, "This? No. I'm a researcher. I specialize in the analysis and translation of ancient documents." He smiled again, held up the chart, and said, "It used to be a lot harder to read these when they were handwritten. Give me a stone tablet anytime."

Georges' pleasant demeanor relaxed Quillon, and he said, "I'm actually glad you're here. I need your help." Quillon glanced at the door then continued, "I want to go home but Doctor 'D' is saying I should remain under observation for a few more days."

Georges tapped the chart and said, "I see." He flipped through a few pages, took a breath, and without looking from the charts said, "It also says," Georges paused, looked at Quillon, "How do I say this? You had a bit of a complication during your blood transfusion."

Quillon felt a tightening of his chest as the memory of that event played through his mind. "That was nothing," said Quillon quickly and a little louder than he had expected. "I fell asleep during the transfusion and had a bad dream. That's it!"

There was a moment of silence, Georges looking at the chart and Quillon feeling embarrassed about his outburst. Finally, Quillon said in a softer voice, "I'm sorry. The dream was nothing. I have had these before."

"Really," said Georges. "Sorry to hear that. From what I read, this one was pretty bad. It says you woke up screaming out your sister's name, and they finally had to sedate you."

"I'm okay now," said Quillon, without looking at Georges. "Believe me, I know how to handle these things. I would really appreciate you speaking with Doctor D. You said they work for you."

"Tell you what. You tell me more about this incident of yours first, then we will talk about what comes next."

"I don't like to talk about my sister or my dreams. Most people don't understand that I know it's not real. I have been struggling with this kind of thing since she died. I'm sure Doctor D knows all about it."

"There was something in here about that," said Georges, waving the chart slightly. "But, as I said, I'm a researcher. A man who is unfortunately motivated by, shall we say, curiosities, and your story interests me."

"I told my dream to Doctor D, and he feels it is related to PTSD."

"I'm not a doctor. I approach things with a different frame of reference. You tell me what happened, and I promise you, I will not make any medical," Georges paused, then said, "or psychological conclusions."

"Where should I start?" said Quillon reluctantly.

"Tell me about the dream first, then about your sister."

"This was not the first dream like this, but it was the most real and the most violent."

"Not the first?" asked Georges.

"In the past, I had dreams, nightmares really, about my sister. But ever since the attack, I have been having nightmares that take place mostly in the library and these differ from those in the past. These feel more real and are filled with much more emotions. The dreams with my sister happened at night. These new dreams come more often, both day and night. If I daydream, it often turns into a nightmare."

"Interesting. Your dreams are both linked to traumatic events. Do you still dream about your sister?" asked Georges, as he pulled up a nearby chair and made himself comfortable.

"Yes, and no," said Quillon. "In the past, she would be the only thing in the dreams, and she would speak to me. Now, she shows up at the end of the dream. In fact, in the past few, she ended the dream. Then, when I wake up, she is standing over me. The last time, she had her hand in my chest and there was a terrible burning all over my chest."

"That's really interesting," said Georges, as he glanced at the chart again. "There is nothing in here about that."

"I guess I was too busy yelling from the pain. When they asked me about it later, I decided not to say anything." Quillon glanced at the door, then said, "I don't want to give them an excuse to keep me here."

Georges leaned forward and asked, "You're saying that your sister actually manifested, in corporeal form, and physically interacted with you?"

Quillon knew from Georges' expression and pitch of his voice he was interested. He worried about answering, because it was questions like that in the past that led to a stay in another type of hospital. He was not sure if he trusted Georges yet, so he said, "I would rather talk about something else."

Georges sat back and said, "I understand. Then let's talk about your nightmares, the more recent ones."

Quillon relaxed a bit. Dreams were dreams, and he had never gotten in trouble for talking about dreams. In fact, his last doctor said they were a healthy way of processing deep seated issues. He studied Georges for a second. He had a slight but disarming smile on his face and appeared honestly interested in what Quillon was saying.

"The dreams about the library," Georges prompted.

"All of them, or just the last one?"

"Did the ones in the past cause you to wake up screaming?" asked Georges.

"No, it was the last one. In fact, that was the worst of them. I can almost feel that dream, like it is a part of me."

Georges pulled out his phone and set it on the table beside Quillon. "You don't mind if I record this part?" When Quillon did not object, Georges started the recorder and signaled for Quillon to start.

"I said that dreams happened in the library, but that isn't actually correct. I'm someplace else and I'm looking through a kind of window at the library. However, the window is in the library. I think it was near the desk, and I can see the entrance."

"Someplace else? You mean like another room?" asked Georges. "Are you in another room looking into the library, like an actual window in the wall?"

"No, I'm sure the window I was looking through is actually in the library." Quillon thought for a second then continued, "It's not really a window, like the normal window. It's more like a round hole. There's some kind of swirling mist that's coming from behind and pouring into it. It's hard to explain, but imagine a drain in the sink, as soap is going down it, but it is vertical, and I don't know where the soap is coming from."

Quillon noticed that Georges' expression had changed from relaxed to concerned as he described the window and he looked deep in thought. "Do you want me to go on?" Quillon asked.

"Yes," said Georges, his smile returning. "Very interesting description. Please continue."

"In the past dreams the hole was too small for me to get through, but in each dream it got bigger. In the last two I could put my arms through it. I remember that the first few times, when it was small, I felt a great anger at not being able to fit through it. I also felt a pain in my chest, near my wound."

"You felt pain during the dream?" asked Georges. The concern look returned to his face.

"I have been feeling pain in my chest a lot lately. They say it is normal. Just my nerves recovering from the shock." Quillon thought for a second then said, "Now that I think about it, I often feel pain right before I find myself in a dream. The pain would continue during the dream, but there were a lot of things I felt, like the cold and emotions, like fear, hate, and worst of all, hunger."

"I can see why PTSD was suggested," said Georges. "You said this last one differed from the past. What made this one so bad?"

Quillon thought about it for a while before answering. He hated to think about that dream, let alone talk about it. There was a lot that was confusing about it. He thought about how to explain it to Georges but decided it was too late to be squeamish now and if it got him out of here, it was worth it. Quillon took a deep breath and said, "I killed a man."

"That's not so bad," said Georges. "I've done the same in some of mine."

"Well, actually, I killed and ate him." When Georges did not reply, Quillon continued. "It was the guy that stabbed me, Hugo. He was standing in the middle of the library, holding that dagger. There were two armed guards at the entrance behind some kind of barrier. There was also another man in a wheelchair yelling instructions to Hugo."

"A man in a wheelchair?' asked Georges. The surprise in his voice was clear. "You're sure you saw a man in a wheelchair?"

Quillon was a little surprised that Georges was asking about the man in the wheelchair and not about Hugo. "Yes. He was in his late fifties and was wearing what looked like a turtleneck and a dark jacket. He was yelling to Hugo, telling him to order the portal closed."

"But you said you killed Hugo, right?"

"Yes," said Quillon, looking down. "When I saw him standing there, it reminded me of when he first attacked me. I could feel an anger growing inside of me. A terrible anger mixed with hate. Stronger than anything I ever felt. So, I reached out and grabbed him."

"You could get through the window and into the library?" asked Georges, with a nervousness in his voice.

"I could only fit a few of my arms through it, but I reached them out and grabbed him. It was horrible. I can still hear Hugo scream, taste his blood. One minute he was there, the next we tore him apart and dragged the pieces of him back into my side of the window."

"Your side?"

"It's like I said. The whole thing felt real. Even now, I'm not sure if I was watching things or doing it."

Georges said nothing. He sat there for a few seconds, then indicated with his hand for Quillon to continue.

"After that, I looked back out the window and saw the dagger laying on the ground, about five or ten feet from the entrance. I felt both hate and fear for that dagger. I also felt a strong pain in my chest. Stronger than I had ever felt before. I could feel my heart beating. The edge of the window also moved with my heart beats. It looked like the window was getting bigger with each pulse. I heard the man in the wheelchair order a guard to get the dagger. I was going to reach for it when I saw Henrietta standing over it. She raised her hand towards me, as if she was telling me to stop, then I felt the burning and itching in my chest. Next thing I knew, I was back in the hospital, but Henrietta was still standing there, her hand in my chest. She said nothing, just stood there staring at me. The burning was so bad that I started screaming and you know the rest."

Quillon closed his eyes. Telling the story took a lot out of him. Just thinking about it brought back all the feelings he had experienced during the dream. It was almost like he was reliving it. He felt his chest itch and placed his hand on it, tapping his finger lightly. Sometimes, just touching it helped when the itch started. Nothing could help when the burning started. He took a deep breath and opened his eyes, wondering how the professor would respond to his story.

To his surprise, the professor was in the hallway near the nurse's station talking on his phone. Quillon hadn't even heard him leave. *Well, there goes any hope of leaving,* he thought. *Another person who thinks I'm crazy. I should have said nothing.*

Georges flashed Quillon a thumbs up sign and hung up the phone. The big smile on Georges' face as he came back into the room had Quillon stumped. He had no clue what Georges' signal or smile could mean.

"Great News," said Georges. The smile on his face seemed genuine. "I took care of everything and you're out of here."

"That's great!" said Quillon. "I really can't thank you enough. When can I leave?" He paused, then said, "I wonder if Glenn can pick me up?"

"You're leaving, but you're not going home," said Georges, still smiling. "I'm having you transferred to my Foundation."

"Your Foundation?" Quillon assumed from the look on Georges' face he thought he was doing Quillon a favor. Quillon did his best to smile and said, "Look, I appreciate your help, but I really want to go home."

"I understand that, and so does your doctor. However, he is insisting that you have a few weeks of observation." Georges stopped, thinking how best to continue. "The only question was, where you were going to spend that time, and this," Georges indicated the room with his hand, "was not one of those places. I offered our services, and he agreed."

"He was going to commit me?" asked Quillon, raising his voice slightly before looking back out into the hallway.

"You and I understand things from a different frame of reference. Others, well, they are less accepting of anything untraditional."

"You're saying you believe what I told you?" asked Quillon. "That I'm not crazy?"

"I'm sure that when you were in our library, you noticed we had a collection of a lot of strange items," said Georges.

Quillon just nodded.

"What do you know of the foundation I work for?"

"Just that you're rich and collect strange stuff."

"I'm the head of the Foundation of the Golden Mean," said Georges. "One of the oldest and most prestigious organization for the study and advancement of magic and other associated practices."

Quillon almost laughed until he saw the look of pride on Georges' face. "You mean like card tricks or like witchcraft?"

Georges waved his hand slightly in front of him and said, "No, nothing as Hollywood as that. We believe in the original meaning of the word, which refers to special or hidden knowledge. In fact, we are the leading authorities in some of the newly appreciated fields, like Metaphysics and Parapsychology."

"You mean like ghosts and such?"

"And such?" said Georges with a chuckle. "And that's why I think it's a good idea for you to come spend some time with us."

"I used to believe in ghosts for a while, that's until I got help. Now I understand that what I thought was Henrietta was just guilt."

"I don't know everything about your past, but I believe what's happening to you now is different. We don't have time to go into details, but I will say that the dagger and the box you opened have a long history. Much of it is unpleasant. I think we could all benefit from spending time together."

Quillon was still upset about the idea of good old Doctor 'D' planning to commit him. "I will not let them do that to me again. There is nothing wrong with me," he muttered.

"I agree. Spend a few weeks with us. We will help you find out what is going on with both your dreams and Henrietta. I promise, when it is done, I will have one of our people produce the paperwork you need to get back to work. Plus, we will pay you for your time with us."

"Okay. I agree. Besides, I have to help you close that box, anyway."

Georges smiled, and as he headed out of the room, he said, "Of course. Just one of many things we need to work on."

As Quillon watched Georges, standing in the hallway talking on his phone, he thought about Henrietta. He accepted she was dead. That her visits in his dreams were his fault. But now things were different. When he saw her after the attack, it was different. She was different. Not like her visits in the past. Now, when she stood before him, hand in his chest, Quillon knew she was real. He could feel himself slipping like last time. Not sure what was real. Things were happening now that he knew he could not run away from. Quillon knew he needed help, and the professor looked like his best option.

Chapter 8
An Expert's Opinion

Georges stood in front of the large monitor on the wall across from his desk watching the activity as a new clear barrier was being attached to the doorway of the library. It looked like a large box laying on its side. The bulk of it sticking into the library with the end of it extending just a few feet into the hallway. Watching the men struggle with it told him it was heavy, but the clear glass look made him worry about how strong it was.

He had watched the video of the attack on Hugo as soon as he returned from his visit with Quillon. It was terrifying. Now he knew what Quillon was trying to tell him. Seeing those large tentacles reach out and rip poor Hugo apart made him worry about the strength of their new barrier.

"You're sure this will hold up to that thing?" It was Yuri's voice and came from one of the three screens on the monitor. The others contained a view of the library and the third, the face of an attractive thin middle-aged woman with short blond hair.

Georges turned his head only slightly as he directed the question to the man standing about four feet behind him and said, "Tell him."

That man was Gregory Stephanus, Head of Security for the Foundation. He was a recent addition to the Foundation, coming from an agency where his history earned him the right to speak face to face with authority, especially in the areas of security.

When he realized Georges would not turn and face him, he took a step closer and said, slowly through a smile, as if talking to a child, "This stuff is almost as strong as steel, but transparent. The military uses it in some of their more special purpose equipment. I wanted it here earlier, but it's hard to get hold of."

"That good?" asked Yuri.

"I would worry more about the surrounding walls and floor, before I worried about that barrier, said Stephanus."

"And are you?" asked Georges. Still watching the monitor, he continued, "worried about the surrounding walls and floors?"

"We're using more traditional supports there, but I felt it would be beneficial to see into the room. That's why I have selected this material."

"I see. If it is so great, why don't we just build a box around the portal?"

"We don't know how big it can expand. Besides, that would require my men to spend time in proximity to that thing."

"Of course, safety first, I understand." Georges continued to study the image on the portal on the screen. The dark burning clouds that defined its borders appeared to fall into the darkness of the portal. The never-ending flow of clouds almost seemed to pull the viewer into its depth.

"It's really quite beautiful. Like looking over the edge of a waterfall," said Yuri. "That is, if you can forget what lies just out of sight."

"It's amazing," said Georges. "Before us is an example of power and level of magic that has been lost to the world for a time unknown."

Regent Elliot, the only other person in the office with Georges and Stephanus, rolled his wheelchair closer to the screen and said, "What I see is a power that would make this foundation the authority it once was. I also see a terrible threat that could destroy us just as easy, if we don't get it under control."

Hearing Elliott's voice broke the peace of mind Georges felt while watching the Portal. He knew it was dangerous, but its movements were almost hypnotic. Georges turned and looked at Elliott. He wished Yuri had made the trip to the foundation. He really did not like being in the same room with Elliott. Georges wished he could find some way to handle this without involving Elliot. In the end, he felt he had no choice because his knowledge of summoning and protection paled compared to Elliot.

"Your experiment with Hugo the other day pointed out just how little we know," said Georges. He turned back to the monitor and continued, "I wish you had waited, or at least discussed it with me, before you tried it. It was a waste of valuable resources."

"I felt the urgency of the situations demanded action." said Elliott. He continued confidently, as if ignoring Georges' comments, "The longer that portal stays open, the greater the danger. Besides, you have admitted that the summoning arts are beyond your area of expertise."

"I may not be as versed in the summoning arts as you but, I know more about this artifact than anyone else. I have been studying it for twenty-five years. I might have been able to provide essential information."

"I'm sorry, Grand Master, but magic is magic," said Elliott. "The history of the event associated with this artifact does not change the basic rules of summoning. It is an accepted fact that the person who holds the instrument of summoning should have power over the spell and those creatures subject to it."

"Well, it is obvious your wielder did not have control. The creature turned him into a mess." Georges looked back at the screen. "Look at that place. It will never be the same. And that rug. It was a gift from my grandfather."

"Then the fault lies with Hugo and not the rules of magic," said Elliot.

As Georges walked back toward his desk, he made sure there was a bit of anger in his voice. He needed to get control of the situation before Elliot took over. "So, you're saying he was not ready? That you didn't prepare him enough? If that's true, it's just another reason for you to coordinate with the team before you act on your own."

"I agree!" said Stephanus. "If I knew how dangerous that creature was, I would have insisted that you wait for the new barrier. You put my men at significant risk."

"That's why your men are here," said Elliott. Turning to Georges, he asked, "Why is he even on this team? He knows nothing of magic! In fact, why are Yuri and his associate part of the team? It should be my people and you."

Georges did his best to control the anger growing inside of him. He glanced back at the monitor in an effort to hide it. He took a few slow breaths, then said, "Yuri is here as an unbiased third party. He represents the other regents. In addition, his department handles all third-party contracts, and he is the liaison with the other societies."

Georges turned to Stephanus and said, "Please inform Regent Elliott of your part in this project."

Stephanus stood with his hands clasped behind his back. He took the time to look at each person, then with an air of authority said, "The man that tried to steal the box and dagger, the one that died in the library, at the hands of that creature, was part of a very successful retrieval group that works out of Europe. His clients include both the rich, some powerful companies and governments. We don't know who hired him. It is unusual for him to work solo. That probably means very few people will be involved. The information he would have needed to plan and attempt the theft could only come from a limited number of people as well."

"Are you saying that Hugo was hired by one of our own?" asked Elliott.

"I will explore all possibilities," said Stephanus.

"I'm still waiting to find out why I'm here," asked the woman on the screen.

"I'm sorry, Doctor Taylor," said Georges. "Gentleman, I would like to introduce you to Doctor Alicia Taylor. She has recently joined us under a contract I just established to expand our studies into the area of Parapsychology. She is, in fact, one of the leading experts in the area. Unfortunately, most of her work was with one of our government partners and is highly confidential."

"I'm surprised, what with my contacts, I haven't heard of you. Or for that fact, of your hiring," said Yuri. "Either way, it's a pleasure to meet you and welcome aboard."

"Thank you. I'm sorry I could not be there in person, but I'm currently speaking at a conference. Which I need to remind you, Professor Georges, limits my time with you. I have studied the information you have sent me on your little problem. I understand why Regent Elliott is a part of this project, but I'm not sure what this creature has to do with my field of Parapsychology?"

"I'm sorry, Doctor Taylor. You're right, it is time to get on with things," said Georges as he pulled out a collection of folders. He slid one towards Elliott and held up one for Stephanus. "I've given both you and Yuri electronic access to the files. I'll have hard copies ready for you, Doctor Taylor, when you get here."

"I prefer electronic," said Taylor.

"The modern way," said Yuri, "I'm afraid I'm a creature of the past. I find paper is much easier to read and does not leave a trail when it is burned."

"That's true, unless it is printed from a computer file," said Taylor with a slight smile of success.

"Can we get on with it!" said Elliott. "You two can trade spy stuff later."

"Patience, Elliott," said Georges with a smile. He was glad to see that Elliott was not making an effort to gain support.

Georges opened the folder and said, "This folder contains information on Quillon, the security guard that was stabbed during the attack. Doctor Demetrio, his attending physician, had some interesting things to report. First, Quillon's wounds were not life threatening, and under normal conditions he would be released after a few days.

However, he has become mildly anemic. Doctor Demetrio said Quillon is having difficulty replacing blood. He said it might have something to do with the dagger fragments which appear to have attached themselves to nearby bone in his rib cage."

"Parts of the dagger?" Elliott's voice did not hide his surprise, or his concern. "How long have you known this?"

"I learned about it when I first visited Quillon in the hospital. I would have gladly shared that knowledge if you had spoken with me before carrying out your experiment."

"I don't understand the problem," said Yuri.

"The dagger was not whole," said Elliott, clearly disturbed by this revelation. "Parts of it are inside Quillon, and I'm sure those parts are feeding off his blood. That means when Hugo went into the library, Quillon was the person wielding the dagger. Hugo never had a chance to command the thing." Elliott paused for a second, then continued, "In fact, Quillon may be acting as both the sacrifice and the summoner."

"Still doesn't involve me," said Taylor. "If you don't need me, I would really like to get back to my symposium."

"Your right. Here is something for you. Yesterday afternoon, I spoke with Quillon. He shared that he's been having several strange dreams or visions. In the most recent of these, he claims to have witness, or as he says, participated in Hugo's murder. He also claimed he saw you Elliott, shouting instructions to Hugo."

"You said he dreamed it," said Taylor. "Any chance he could have overheard talk about it?"

Georges shook his head and said, "He provided details that clearly proved he was a witness."

"Interesting," said Taylor. "You said he reported both witnessing and taking part in the attack?"

"He was very confused, and his retelling shifted back and forth between seeing the attack and being the attacker. He said he experienced the sounds, smells, and feelings of the attack."

"You're sure he mentioned sensory association?" asked Taylor.

"Yes, but there is more," said Georges. "He also said that the ghost of his dead sister is involved. She was present after a few of the attacks, and Quillon reported she has been hurting him."

"Hurting him. How?"

"He said each time he wakes from one of these dreams, his sister is standing over him. In the last dream, the one with Hugo, he woke to find her with her hand in his chest. He felt a burning and itching sensation which he thinks was causing the rash on his chest."

"PS&N," Taylor's face brightened as she said, "This is getting interesting."

"PS&N?" asked Yuri.

"Sorry. Trade slang for Parapsychology and Paranormal." Taylor paused for a moment, as if considering something, then said, "Professor, I will take the job. I'll send my assistant there tomorrow to handle moving my equipment."

"I'm sorry?" said Georges. A bit taken aback by Taylor's offer. He was just about to remind her he had already hired her, and she worked for him, when Stephanus interrupted.

"I'll need background information on your assistant."

"I'm not sure we should add anyone else to this project, Doctor Taylor," said Georges, trying to regain control of the conversation.

"I wouldn't have suggested it if I didn't need him. Don't worry, his clearance is probably higher than any of yours," said Taylor, no longer looking at the screen as she busily made notes. "Should I have him coordinate with you Stephanus on logistics?"

"That will be fine." said Stephanus, making a quick note in a small black notebook he pulled from a pocket inside his jacket.

"Can we please get back to the project?" said Georges, glancing at Stephanus as if challenging him to continue.

Georges could not help but see the holstered weapon peeking out from under Stephanus's jacket as he returned his notebook to its place.

Georges quickly looked away, returned his attention to Taylor expecting to hear more from her, and was surprised when Elliott asked, "Are these photographs of the rash?"

"Yes, Doctor Demetrio reported it is common to have bruising after surgery. At first, he was worried about infection, but they ruled that out. What surprised him was the bruising was forming distinct patterns. Doctor Demetrio believes the patterns are caused by blood capillaries near the skin. He described it as something like a tattoo drawn in blood instead of ink."

"The Doctor's description is very good," said Elliott as he spread the pictures out on the desk. "I have seen something like this before. In some places, it is called a blood curse or hex, but they normally draw it on someone with the blood of a victim. I have also heard of cases where it was claimed to be protective in nature."

"I've never heard of it before," said Georges. "You're saying they can be used for both cursing and protecting?"

"It's common to use many symbols in summoning and spell casting. Sometimes these are painted on bodies or other surfaces. There are a few stories of symbols being carved into a person's skin. These are referred to as blood tattoos. I'm surprised you didn't come across that in your studies."

Georges didn't respond to Elliott's comment. He stared at the pictures, then went to his safe and retrieved the box. As he set it on the desk, he said, "I think it's time we bring this into our discussion."

Elliott rolled closer to the desk. As he reached for the box, he hesitated, then said, "Is the dagger inside?"

"Yes, and as you can see, the box is not fully closed, so be careful," said Georges handing Elliott the box.

"Amazing," said Elliott as he examined it. "What is it made of? It's not wood."

"We aren't sure, maybe bone, but the thing I want to point out is how closely the pattern on the box matches those of Quillon's rash or tattoo."

Both Georges and Elliott studied the box. While the images in the photograph did not match exactly, the resemblance to those on the box was clear. There was an uncomfortable silence as they stared at the box.

It was Taylor who spoke next. "I'm sure what you're looking at is interesting, but I have some questions about how best to proceed. How stable is Quillon?"

"Doctor Demetrio feels he is on the verge of a breakdown and recommends he be committed for a period of observation and, if necessary, treatment. Demetrio said Quillon's medical records suggested this has happened before, shortly after his sister's death."

"And how was he when you talked to him?" asked Taylor

"He was hesitant to talk at first, but once I convinced him I was on his side, he opened up about the dreams. They upset him, but he said he knew how to handle them. I think that was a bit of brave talk," said Georges.

"And his sister, the ghost. What's the story there?" asked Taylor, busily making notes.

"He really didn't want to talk much about her," said Georges. "I got an understanding that what was happening now differs from the past, and that has him worried."

"Very interesting," said Taylor. "I think we should focus first on his visions of his sister. I'm not sure how he would react if he learned his dreams were true."

"I'm not worried about hurting his feelings," said Elliott. "Have we forgotten what is waiting for us in the library?"

"I agree, this is scary stuff, very much your kind of business," said Taylor. "However, what's happening to Quillon is more my business. The mind is a fragile thing. Break it and we both lose. Seeing you, the man in his dreams, might be too much for him right now."

"I agree with her," said Georges. "Let's give her some time with him before we introduce him to you."

"I disagree," said Elliott. "This is my area of expertise, and I don't really think exploring Quillon's dreams is necessary. It's his role as the summoner and the victim that is important. What we need to do is finish the ritual."

"And how are you suggesting we do that?" asked Georges, knowing the answer before he asked.

"If he dies by the blade, the summoning is complete. The person who finishes the ceremony should then be able to control the creature." Elliot spoke in a matter-of-fact way, as if there was no way to challenge his statement.

"And who do you suggest we get to finish the job?" asked Yuri. "Are you volunteering?"

"I'm sure we can dig up someone with nothing to lose, who we can convince to do the job," said Elliott, with a soft chuckle, as he opened the box and looked at the dagger inside.

"I know this is not my field, but I don't understand the relationship between the creature, the portal, and Quillon. It sounds more complex than the simple summoning that you suggest. I think it would be a shame to waste an opportunity to study these phenomena," said Taylor.

Elliott rolled his chair back from the desk to give him space. He pointed toward the monitor on the wall. The anger in his voice was clear when he said, "I'm sorry, Doctor Taylor, but your trivial pursuits are meaningless compared to the power and danger that is waiting in that room. We are looking at a lost magic. Possibly the most powerful magic on earth." Elliott turned his chair to face Georges and said, "We should be prepared to do whatever it takes for us to get control of that magic. I'm asking you, Grand Master, where are your loyalties, with the Foundation or your nobody security guard?"

Georges could see the anger growing in Elliot's face. Georges had struggled through the meeting to resist Elliot's barbs but could not let that last one go unchallenged.

"My goals are the same as yours, Regent Elliott!" said Georges. "I'm afraid there is more going on here than we understand. Before I take drastic action, I want to be sure it will work!"

To Georges' surprise, Elliott laughed and said, "Magic always works. We both know that. Even with your knowledge of the subject, I think we can both agree that the longer we wait, the more we risk losing control."

"I will not rush into this," said Georges sternly. "I feel that there are opportunities to get what we want using Doctor Taylor's methods, and I will not change my mind!"

"Your wrong! I will take this to the other regents. They'll see my way is best for the Foundation," said Elliott.

"Regent Elliott, I need to remind you that the details of this project are restricted to the members of the team only," said Stephanus, now standing in front of the office door. "I cannot allow you to break those security restrictions and remain on the team."

"You, cannot allow it?" said Elliott, raising his voice. "I'm a regent! One word from me and you're gone. Now, get out of my way."

When Stephanus did not move, Georges smiled and said, "I have given Stephanus full control over the security of this project."

Elliot glared at Georges and said, "Get out of my way!" and rolled toward the door.

"Since you have decided to leave of your own accord, I have no choice but to remove you from this project," said Georges. "Doctor, we will be relying on you."

Elliott paused at the door for a second.

"Stephanus, please see Regent Elliot out. Then arrange for Quillon to be brought here. Put him someplace safe, and make sure he is not disturbed by anyone, and I mean anyone not on the project access list."

Stephanus smiled as he held the door for Regent Elliot. This was part of the job he liked. He had been listening quietly, trying to see where he would fit into this thing. He was not disturbed at talks of violence. In fact, he considered it an expected part of his profession; something he was good at. What he didn't like was being told how to be violent. He was not fond of the Grand Master, but the one thing he appreciated was his instructions were just vague enough for Stephanus to do things how he thought best. As he followed Elliott through the door, his thoughts were on how best to carry out the Grand Master's last orders.

Chapter 9
The New VIP

Quillon felt a little uncomfortable as he sat in the large luxurious car that was taking him back to the Foundation. It was not because of his injuries. They made every effort to prevent that. It was not the idea of returning to the scene of his attack. He was honestly curious if things would look like his dreams, or like the last time he saw it. What made him uncomfortable was sitting across from Stephanus.

Quillon remembered the night of the party, when Stephanus had introduced himself as the head of security. He had made it clear that Quillon and his coworkers were there as window dressing. As pacifiers, to calm any nervous guests.

It ruffled Quillon's feathers a bit. He remembered Glenn joking about Stephanus as they were being led to the party area. "I didn't think someone could wear that much black. I can't decide if he dresses like a tough guy from a movie, or the tough guys in the movies are dressing like him."

Quillon smiled at that memory, but his smile quickly faded, as he noticed Stephanus watching him, still dressed in a black suit, just like the night of the party.

They had been traveling at least twenty minutes and Stephanus had spoken less than ten words. He just sat there watching as Quillon signed papers after papers pushed his way by two other men, dressed in nicer, friendlier suits. They would summarize each document and then show Quillon where to sign. There was one for the hospital, one for his salary while helping the Foundation, another promising not to sue the foundation, and finally one that said the Foundation had the rights to all intellectual or physical artifacts created or discovered during his time with the foundation.

It was a relief when the papers stopped coming his way. Quillon gave his hand a little shake, like it was cramped, smiled and said, "I'm glad I didn't have to sign those in blood."

Quillon saw the hint of a smile on Stephanus' face, just before the big man turned and looked out the window. Hoping that now was a good time to ask questions, Quillon said, "The Professor said nothing about how long I'm going to stay, or even where I'm going to stay. Do you know?"

Stephanus looked back at Quillon, this time he smiled. He then calmly said, "How long, is a hotly debated question. But don't worry. I have made arrangements for your housing."

That didn't really answer Quillon's questions. Stephanus continued to watch Quillon as if daring him to ask something else.

Quillon stared out the window, watching the scenery go by. His last visit had been in the evening, but the view was much the same in the daylight. Trees, lots and lots of trees. He had heard the Foundation sat in the center of a large, wooded area, almost 20 acres, but driving through it made it seem larger. Glenn had said there was supposed to be a small village on the property where most of the employees lived. *That could be nice,* he thought. *Kind of like a vacation village.*

Quillon was thinking of asking if that was where he was going to stay when Stephanus said, "We're here."

As they came around a small curve, Quillon could see a stone fence and impressive gate house. Beyond that, a collection of buildings, almost like a college campus, with one larger than the other. That building was one of those modern designs from the sixties. It reminded Quillon of a collection of stacked cubes with long thin pillars that ran from ground to the roof and looked more like vertical venetian blinds. It was also the building where he'd been attacked. The last time he was here, it was all lit up with lights for the party and there was a line of limos in front of it. Today, without those lights, it seemed darker, less friendly.

The gate opened automatically as they passed. He remembered how long it had taken to get past that gate on his last visit. The phone calls for clearance, the checks inside and under the vehicle, and the frisking to make sure no one was carrying a weapon. "It's nice to be the boss," said Quillon, with a smile toward Stephanus, and was surprised to see he got one back.

Sitting back, Quillon studied the front of the building and thought about what was waiting for him. Suddenly, he noticed the car was turning and heading toward the back of the building where deliveries were made. It was the same way they forced Glenn to take that night. "Hey, why are we turning?" he asked.

Without looking at Quillon, Stephanus said, "This way is safer." He then used a small handheld radio and said, "On approach."

Safer? From what? thought Quillon. He was thinking about asking, but didn't. He'd worked with a few officers in the past, those with military experience, and they all got a kind of look in their eyes when they were gearing up for something. Stephanus had that look, and Quillon knew he would not get any answers right now.

Pulling into the loading area, Quillon saw twelve men, all dressed in dark suits. There were four on the road level, four on the landing dock, and another four near the entrance. He noticed there were no other vehicles in the area, unlike that last time when it was cluttered with deliveries for the party.

Things after that happened quickly. He was out of the car, up the ramp stairs, and into a waiting elevator before he realized it. Half the time, he was being encouraged to move by one or more of the black-suited men, as they securely and a few times, less than gently guided him by his arm.

From the outside, it was difficult to know how many floors the building had. Now that he was in an elevator, he could see from the panel there were four upper floors and three basement levels. The floor buttons were dark, but when Stephanus tapped a card against a panel, they all lit up. Quillon was a little concerned when Stephanus pressed the button labeled B3.

"Where are we going?" ask Quillon nervously.

"Your apartment," responded Stephanus.

"I'm going to stay in the basement?" asked Quillon nervously. "I thought I might get to stay in the village."

"You'll like this more. It's closer to the action. Easier for you to get your work done," said Stephanus, looking straight ahead.

Quillon thought he saw a slight smirk on Stephanus' face and was relieved when the door opened to reveal a brightly lit space, not the dark dungeon he was imagining.

The hallway was wider than normal and was tiled in a nice blue and white checkered pattern, with flakes of gold in it. To the right, down the hallway, he saw two doors. There was one on each side of the hallway. To the left, he saw large, windowed areas on each side. In one, he saw tables and chairs. In the other, he saw a few old fashion arcade machines. He also noticed that there were no painting, plants, or decorations of any kind anywhere.

Across from the elevator was a little room with a half door. There were two officers inside and another just outside. These were dressed in uniforms, unlike the guys in black suits, and had tasers on their belt. They stared at Quillon, Stephanus and the two black-suited men in the elevator like they had just been caught doing something wrong.

Stephanus stepped out and said, "Gentleman, we have a VIP with us for a while. Treat him with respect, and make sure you review your post orders."

"You're going to like this place," said Stephanus, putting his hand on Quillon's shoulder. "It has everything you need. There is a cafeteria over there," he said, pointing toward the room with tables. "And we even installed a few of your favorite video games." Stephanus pointed toward the room with the arcade machines. "If we're wrong about them, you can blame your boss."

What kind of VIP's stay here? thought Quillon. *This feels more like a bomb shelter,* as he looked around.

He could feel the officers studying him, wondering how much his appearance was going to change their routine. Quillon had been in that spot before. He smiled, gave a small wave, and said, "I guess you guys got the good post," pointing toward the game room. He could feel the tension lessen a bit. It returned the moment Stephanus spoke.

"Now, it's time for my guys to check you in," said Stephanus, pointing toward the little room in front of him. "I'm afraid you will have to turn in your cellphone."

"Why?" asked Quillon as he pulled it from his pocket.

"Security reasons. Besides, nothing works down here. It's designed that way," said Stephanus, as he took Quillon's phone and handed it to the officer behind the counter. "You'll get it back when you leave."

Quillon had been without his phone before. Each time he had spent some time in treatment, they made him surrender it. Looking around, he got a chill as those old memories returned.

"The passkey they'll give you operates your room door, plus the arcade and vending machine. Loose it and you won't be able to get out of here," Stephanus said with a smile. "That's a little security humor. I'm sure you can appreciate it."

Quillon didn't, but smiled, pretending it was funny. He saw the officer issuing the pass do the same. He hung the pass around his neck and followed his black suited escorts down the hall, stopping in front of the door on the left.

"This will be your new home while you are with us." Stephanus pointed to a white plastic panel on the wall and said, "Tap your card here to open it."

Quillon nodded, and said, "Got it. What's next?"

Stephanus said nothing. It took Quillon a few seconds to understand that Stephanus was not explaining things, but giving instruction he expected Quillon to follow. He took the pass from around his neck and tap the panel. The door slid open a little quicker than Quillon expected. He had assumed it would just unlock and then he could open it. Now that he studied the door, he noticed there wasn't a doorknob. Quillon tapped the panel again, and the door whooshed closed. "Hey, that's cool. Just like on Star Trek." He opened the door again. Now that the shock factor had worn off, he noticed the room interior.

"Go in. Look around," said Stephanus, his arm pointing toward the room.

Quillon did and was impressed by the size of the room. He guessed it took up the whole side of the floor, at least up to the security shack. It was divided into three areas: a bedroom, a bathroom, and a sitting area. He could not imagine what good the sitting area would be without a TV or even a book to read. As he was looking around, he noticed it was missing a few things. "There are no walls," he said. Glancing at the bathroom, he added, "and there are no doors. Even the closet doesn't have a door."

"Yes," said Stephanus, as if it had settled the question. He turned and headed toward the door, tapping on a set of controls there. "If you need anything, this is an intercom. You'll also find the controls for the lights here. I'm sorry but, the nightlight built into this unit can't be turned off. Safety Reasons. I'm sure you understand."

"Wait," said Quillon, stepping toward Stephanus. "My stuff, I need my stuff. My clothes and my pills."

"We have provided everything you'll need. You'll find your pills in the bathroom and clothes in the closet," Stephanus said, pointing toward a doorless closet next to the bathroom. "Just leave the dirty items in the basket in the bathroom."

Quillon walked over to the closet and picked up a tee-shirt. "They're white," he said. Looking down, he saw a pair of white slippers. "Why is everything white?"

"Some of our guests in the past had issues with dyes or fragrances."

Putting the shirt back, Quillon asked, "When do I get to meet with Professor Georges?"

"Unfortunately, the professor is in meetings today. He suggested you get a good night's sleep," said Stephanus as he stepped into the hallway. "He'll meet with you tomorrow. The professor is very eager to introduce you to Doctor Taylor."

"Who is Doctor Taylor?" asked Quillon in a worried tone.

Stephanus reached up, and just before he tapped the door panel, he smiled and said, "She's someone that really wants to meet your sister."

Quillon stood staring at the closed door, wondering if he had heard Stephanus right.

Chapter 10
Wake-up Call

Quillon slept like a baby. He had expected the strange, windowless surrounding would have kept him awake. Instead, it made him realize just how loud his apartment was. The king-size bed helped a lot. He would have been glad to spend a few more hours in it, but the soft beeping of an alarm got his attention. The small LED on the intercom by the door was blinking a soft pink with each beep.

Quillon stumbled across the room toward it. The little light went out the moment he touched it. A light ding followed shortly after it. He was not sure what to do, so he just said, "Hello?"

"Mr. Thomas, this is your wake-up call. Food is being served in the cafeteria for the next hour," came a voice through the intercom.

"Thanks," said Quillon. "I'll be there just as soon as I shower and get dressed."

There was no reply from the intercom.

"Hello, did you hear me?" asked Quillon. There was no response. *Must be a recording,* he thought. *I wonder how old that recording is.* He looked around for a clock but couldn't find one. *I hope I didn't miss breakfast.*

Quillon quickly showered and dressed in the clothes provided for him. White sweatpants, tee shirt, and slippers. He was thankful he did not have to wear a bathrobe. That would have made him feel too much like he was back in a hospital.

He stepped out into the hallway and could not resist playing with the door a few times. When he noticed he was being watched by the officers down the hall, he just smiled and said, "I need to get one of these for my place," and headed toward them.

He smiled at the two officers and, for the first time since he got here, he felt at home. "Did I miss chow?" he asked.

One of them pointed toward the food line and said, "It's self-serve. Get it while you can."

Quillon made his way to the cafeteria and saw another officer eating there. He had a red stripe on his shoulder epaulet, so Quillon figured he was their shift supervisor. Quillon made his way to the food line and was surprised at the amount of food. "Someone else joining us?" he asked.

"Next shift will be here in a few," said the seated officer. "You're lucky you got here when you did. They're a bunch of chow hounds."

"You guys got it pretty sweet here. My company's got me working an overnight post. No free food there. In fact, I'm lucky if the vending machines work."

"Yeah, we heard about you and your buddies," the man said with a chuckle.

"All good, I'm sure," said Quillon.

"Name's Morgan. I'd love to talk shop, but the boss said to minimize contact with you for security reasons." He stood up, dropped off his tray, and headed out of the cafeteria. Before leaving, Morgan said, "You got about ten minutes before someone is coming to escort you to your first meeting."

"Thanks," said Quillon, as he looked down at his tray. *Not much time,* he thought, and had a seat. He had mixed feelings about this place. Quillon was glad that someone believed him, and he was really glad about the idea of getting paid for nothing. He did not know how long it was going to be before he got back to work.

The food was good. He didn't realize how hungry he was. He was thinking about going back for seconds when he heard someone behind him.

"Time to go."

Quillon glanced behind him and saw a uniformed officer standing there. "Okay," he said, shoving another fork full of pancakes into his mouth. "Just give me a second to finish this."

"Now!" said the officer. "Leave your tray."

Fork in hand, Quillon turned, ready to tell the officer off, then he laughed instead. "Newbie," he shouted and got up. "It's nice to see someone I know."

The officer only scowled at Quillon.

"Remember me? The library?" Quillon paused for a second then said, "Hey, what happened to your dark suit?"

"You happened!" said the officer, not bothering to hide his feelings.

"Me?" asked Quillon, dropping his fork and wiping his face. "Why me?"

"They blamed me for what happened. Said the attacker got past me."

"Tough break," said Quillon. "But it's true."

The officer took a step forward, poked his finger in Quillon's chest and said, "Watching the library was your job. I took the fall because you couldn't do your job."

Quillon slapped the officer's finger away and was getting ready to walk past the man when the fist hit his face. He fell backward against the table. He tried to break his fall, but his injured arm did not move fast enough.

The next thing he knew, he was on the floor looking up. His head hurt, and so did his arm. As he laid there, he felt a sharp pain coming from the area of his wound. He pressed his chest with his other hand, hoping to stop the pain. It only increased. He took a breath, looked up, and saw a group of officers standing around him. Their expressions worried him. He looked at his hand and was surprised to see blood on it. He looked at his chest where his hand had been and saw blood there, too.

"You okay?" asked Morgan, who was standing near him. When Quillon did not answer, Morgan said, "Don't move. I'll get some help."

Quillon nodded while staring at his hand. It was strange. He expected more pain. The red spot on his chest had grown a little and as he stared at it, a strange smell reached his nose. A kind of metallic smell, which somehow, he knew, was the smell of his own blood. The smell grew stronger, and he cleared his throat several times. Each time, he felt a pain deep in his chest. It started small, like a sore muscle ache, but soon it turned into a sharp biting pain that almost pulsed.

He placed his hand back over the bloodstain and pressed, hoping to hold back the pain. As he pressed, he felt an itch and a burning.

Someone was speaking to him, but the sharp pain and the burning were all he could focus on. The two pains grew stronger, almost like they were competing. Soon, the sharp pain was all he could think of. That pain and the smell of blood. He felt the room spin. He turned his head left and right, trying to stop it. That only made it worse. His eyes felt heavier and heavier. Soon he could not resist their weight and closed his eyes.

Chapter 11
Act of Anger

When Quillon opened his eyes again, the pain was almost gone. Around him was the familiar unworldly surrounding of his past dreams.

This time, it felt different. During his past visits, it felt real, but this was different. It felt, well, normal. On the other visits, he always felt like he was looking through a haze. Sometimes he would hear things; sometimes he could smell things. This time, all his senses were active. He also noticed that the small window that he had watched through before was larger. He felt like he had more wiggle room; a freedom he had not felt before. Quillon felt himself stretching and taking deep breaths of an air that he somehow knew smelled different from what he had been breathing moments before.

Movement caught his attention, and he turned to see two men in tactical outfits standing in the doorway of the library behind what looked like a clear barrier. It was kind of like a box on its side that allowed access into the room from one side.

The outfits they were wearing covered most of their faces, but he could definitely see the look of panic in the wide eyes that were locked on him. Their stance also worried him. He didn't have any military training, but it was clear these men had.

Quillon raised his hands in an effort to calm them, but their response was the opposite of what he had expected. One man had positioned himself at the side of the barrier that allowed access to the room. He had his gun braced against the edge of the barrier for support. Quillon caught a quick flash of a laser that he was sure was now directed somewhere on him. The other man was on the radio, shouting something about being under attack.

Instead of fear, Quillon felt anger. Something that was not typical for him. He tried to move toward the men, but felt something holding him back. He realized it was the little window he watched this world through. Quillon could only fit partly through it. It was clear by the sound of a shot being fired in his direction that the two guards did not realize the limitation of his movements.

Quillon pulled back inside the little window. He had felt no pain from the gunfire, so decided it was a warning shot. He hoped that his retreat would calm the guards, but he could see that their positions and, more importantly, their aggressive attitude had not changed.

The anger he had felt earlier continued to grow inside him. Quillon felt his arms tense and, to his surprise, he lunged at the men, but his effort was stopped by the clear barrier.

The attack took the two men by surprise. They retreated fully behind the barrier but did not run. Their trust in the barrier was clear when one of them lowered his gun and returned to talking on the radio.

Quillon felt himself pull back, tense up, and he lunge at the barrier again. This time, he focused his attack at a single point. He saw the expressions of terror on the faces of the men just before he felt the window give way. The force of the attack and the shattering plastic forced both men back and to the ground. Quillon could see the closest man hold up his hands, attempting to fight back against the falling debris that quickly trapped him under its weight.

The other guard pushed his way out from under some of the smaller pieces of plastic and looked around. Seeing his trapped comrade, he made a few useless attempts to free him. Unsuccessful, he looked around and saw the gun he had dropped, just about the same time as Quillon. The guard reached for it but was quickly yanked away from it by a long slimy tentacle wrapped around his leg. The man was raised up by his leg and held in place, with his head just inches from the ground, his arms flailing around.

Quillon could feel a sense of anger mixed with something else. A strong hunger. He could almost smell the blood dripping from the wound on the dangling man's face. Soon he forgot the man's screaming and his focus was only on the blood. He heard movement and felt the stirring of his arms, followed by the sound of grumbling. His mind filled with smells so strong it sickened him. There was also a voice calling out for food. He could hear the gnashing of teeth and overwhelming waves of hunger. He felt himself reaching for the dangling man and saw several long, slimy appendages skirting around the floor. Some long and thin, other short and fat, like a collection of worms racing for a prize.

Quillon watched as the arms climbed up the dangling man, many pulling pieces as they did, then quickly retreating, clutching their prize. Soon there was nothing left but a stain on the floor above where the man had hung, along with a few pieces that had been dropped in haste. A few final arms reached out to absorb the puddles of blood.

Quillon felt sick, helpless. He could stop nothing that had just happened. First, it was like he was watching a horror movie, but soon he felt as if he had become part of it. An unwilling contributor held captive by the emotions that almost overwhelmed him. Now that it was over, he was thankful for the quiet. Well, there was still the moaning from the man trapped under the debris, but the voices in his head had stopped.

He closed his eyes, put the sound of the man out of his head and rested in the peaceful quiet that remained. It was then that he felt something hit him in the face. It surprised him. He opened his eyes and looked around for his attacker, but could see no one. Seconds later, the pain returned. This time, it was so painful that he closed his eyes. Confused, he did not know what to do next. With the next sharp pain, he also heard his name being called. He kept his eyes shut out of fear.

He felt dizzy, and he heard his name again. This time, he opened his eyes and looked around.

It took a few seconds to realize that he was not in the library. Quillon blinked and did his best to focus his vision on the faces that surrounded him. He recognized the uniforms of the security. Glancing around further, he saw Professor Georges, Stephanus and a woman with short blond hair he guessed was a nurse. The expressions on their faces worried him a bit, but he was glad to see someone he knew. That meant it had all been a dream.

The memory of past dreams reminded that someone was missing from the little group. In the past, the pain that Henrietta brought would replace the drama of the dream. He glanced around the room, fearing that pain. He sighed in relief when he did not see her.

"Are you okay?"

It was the professor's voice. Quillon, still looking at the ceiling, said, "Another terrible dream. This one was the worst so far." He turned in the professor's direction and any remaining words failed him as he saw Henrietta step through the professor, her hand outreached, as she advanced slowly towards him.

"No, get away from me!" Quillon shouted, shaking his head. He tried to get up but felt the pressure on his shoulder as someone held him down. While he heard a chorus of people telling him to calm down, relax, or he would hurt himself, Henrietta continued her advance.

All Quillon could do was yell, "No, don't! Please, don't hurt me, Henrietta," as she walked through the group that was holding him and placed her hand on his chest.

The touch of her hand was cold, but the burning that followed was not. It spread through his chest. Besides the pain, he felt an itching that crawled from his wound out in all directions. He felt it making its way up his neck, towards his arm, around his side, and toward his stomach.

Quillon closed his eyes and screamed, then as quick as it had started, it stopped. Only the slight tingle on his skin remained. He opened his eyes and Henrietta was gone. The pressure on his shoulder was gone as well. He looked around at the surprise on the faces that surrounded him.

Weakly, he continued to look amongst the faces for Henrietta. In relief, he said, "She's gone." Shaking his head, he said, "Why Henrietta? Why do you always hurt me? I'm sorry. I really am. Please Henrietta, no more."

"Put him out," came the voice of the professor.

Quillon felt the pressure on his shoulders as two security men held him down. He felt a sharp pain in his arm, and a warm feeling that made its way through his body followed by a muffling of sound and finally a darkness.

Chapter 12

Get Serious

Georges watched as they placed Quillon on a stretcher and carried it down the hallway to the elevator. The Foundation had a little clinic on the first floor. Nothing fancy; it was intended to handle minor injuries. It had turned into more of a pharmacy. Plus, it handled requests for some of the more specialized herbs and ingredients needed by a few of the more exotic departments. Georges was sure it could handle monitoring Quillon until he woke up.

He had arrived on the scene shortly after Taylor, whose new office was much closer. It didn't take long for the word about Quillon's breakdown to reach other areas of the Foundation. Both Elliott and Stephanus exited the elevator that Quillon soon occupied.

Georges raised his hand toward Elliott to stop any comments from him. He turned to Stephanus and asked, "How bad is it?"

"One dead, another trapped under that shielding. My guess is he also won't make it."

"What started it?" asked Georges.

"One of my men and Quillon got into a scuffle," said Stephanus. "Quillon was injured, and that appears to be when he had his episode."

"And the library?" asked Georges.

"It's not clear what happened there. My men made a call that they were under attack. When the backup got there, the creature had retreated into the portal. I will know more once I see the video."

Georges nodded and said, "I'm sorry about your men. Do what you need to improve the barrier."

As Stephanus walked away, Elliott said, "What we need to do is close the portal. You insisted that Doctor Taylor would achieve that goal."

Elliott turned his chair toward Taylor, as if expecting her to respond to his statement. Instead, she calmly said, "I'm sorry, Regent, but it is my understanding that you're not on the distribution list for project status reports."

The tightness in Elliott's lips showed her comments had the impact she intended. Before Elliott could explode, Georges said, "We are making progress. I will give Yuri a full briefing after this."

Elliott turned his chair toward Georges, dramatically, and said, "You had your shot. I'm calling for an emergency meeting of the Regents. It's time to get serious about this threat before anyone else gets hurt."

"Then I will see you at the meeting. In the meantime, we have work to do here." Georges turned to one of the security officers standing nearby and said, "Please press the elevator call button for Regent Elliot."

"Stay where you are!" said Elliott, who gave Georges an icy stare before moving his chair toward the elevators.

Georges knew he had probably gone too far on that last comment, but right now he wanted to get rid of Elliott so he could ask those same questions to Doctor Taylor. He looked at Taylor, indicated with his head toward the far end of the cafeteria behind her, and walked that way. Georges asked the officers straightening up the area to find someplace else to be for a while. They nodded and quickly left.

Making his way over to the drink dispenser, Georges filled a glass with lemonade. "You want some?" He asked, not really expecting her to agree.

"Half ice-tea, half lemonade. Light on the ice, please."

George smiled, then said, "Elliott's right, you know." He topped off her glass and offered it to her.

"I agree, but you're asking me to solve this problem with very limited information. In fact, I haven't even met with Quillon." She took a sip, put the glass down, and said, "Too much lemonade."

"I understand," said Georges. "I'm asking you to give me something. Anything that I can take to the council. I don't even care if it's right!" said Georges as he walked over to one of the nearby tables. "Unless I can counter Elliott's claims, you will be lucky if you can get a job delivering phone books."

"I didn't know they still delivered phone books," said Taylor.

"Exactly. Now, tell me something I can use."

Taylor joined Georges at the table, sat down, and pulled out her phone. She flipped through a few screens, then said, "Based on Quillon's comments a few minutes ago, he still thinks the dreams are just dreams. His primary concern is his sister, who's visits, he is convinced, are real. I'm sure guilt fuels part of that. I have done some background research, and he's had several years of therapy, complete with a few brief visits to a psychiatric hospital, plus a suicide attempt."

"He's a troubled man, I get it. But how does that help us with our problem?"

"I think there are two different agents at work here. Both real, regardless of what Quillon thinks. Both with their own objectives, not necessarily mutual ones." Taylor paused for a second, then continued, "In fact, it's quite possible they are working against each other."

"Okay, we are facing ghosts and nightmares. How does that help us?"

"I'm not ready to say ghosts. There were none of the environmental markers that typically accompany a spectral manifestation. It was clear he was interacting with something, and that something is having both a mental and physical impact, unlike his dreams. I'm not sure if you noticed, but during all his screaming, he was clawing at his chest and telling his sister to stop hurting him. It is my bet that if we examine him now, we will find his rash, or tattoo, has grown. Why and what it means, it is too early to tell."

"And his dreams?" asked Georges, surprised he had missed what now seemed obvious.

"Each has become more violent, both physical and emotional. I'm going to guess that he is connecting with the creature, almost merging with it. I have also noticed that the portal has expanded with each attack."

Once again, the things were there before him, and he missed them. He felt old. "That's impressive, doctor, but that brings us back to why I brought you into this. Tell me how we can use this to get what we want."

"Let me continue with my studies," said Taylor, making a note on her phone. "First, we need to find out how both agents are communicating with Quillon. Then, I want to see if there is some way to block them or use it to our advantage. I may also need to run some simple medical tests."

"Fine," said Georges. "However, he does not leave the Facility. You can have Doctor Demetrio run analysis. We will get a portable unit brought in if you need anything stronger than an x-ray."

"I'll have a talk with Quillon once he wakes up. Hopefully that will give me a better understand of what just happened," said Taylor as she walked back to the drink fountain and fixed her drink. Took a sip, smiled, and walked back to stand near Georges.

"I want reports every day, twice a day, if possible. My guess is we have about two days before Elliott can convince the Regents to meet now, instead of in a week as planned. We need you to get serious about this. Tell me what you need, and you'll have it."

Taylor took another sip, and said, "Understood," then walked down the hallway toward the elevator.

Georges, still sitting, turned his back toward the elevator, and quickly added something to his drink from a small flask he kept in his jacket pocket. He heard the soft ding of the elevator and turned to see Taylor glancing his way, a smile on her face, just before she stepped in.

Georges was sure she had seen nothing. Even if she did, these were stressful times. He tapped the container in his coat pocket and thought about everything that Taylor had said. Most of it, he realized, did not require a degree in parapsychology. He was sure that Elliot probably picked up on most of the same things she did. The question now was, how would Elliott use it to hurt him and get the council to decide he was a better choice to manage this project, and possibly the position of Grand Master. Georges hated to admit it, but things might have been easier to manage if Elliott had stayed on the team.

He downed his drink and headed toward the elevator. He had spent the past two days studying all the notes on the Necro Box and something that Taylor said stuck in his mind. Two agents working toward their own objectives. "It couldn't be that simple," he said out loud.

Georges knew Elliott was driven by both his lust for power and his desire to hurt Georges. He needed to find a false lead that Elliott could grab and run with. Something that would make him look foolish. It would not finish Elliott, but it would give him a little more time to find something to tell the council.

Georges glanced at his watch. He had a lunch meeting scheduled with some people from the Metaphysical department he hoped could help him on a personal level. He thought about calling it off, but decided his health came first and pushed the elevator call button.

Chapter 13
Dead, Like Not Alive

Quillon didn't recognize the ceiling. Experience, however, had taught him enough to know when he was in a medical facility. *Not again,* he thought. He tried to clear his mind and remember how he got here. His head hurt and he didn't remember going to sleep. As he placed his hand on his head, he heard someone behind him say, "I was worried you were going to sleep all day."

It was a woman's voice. Quillon attempted to roll toward the voice and was rewarded with a sharp pain in his chest. He laid back, held his breath for a few seconds, and worked through the pain. Looking at his chest, he saw a large bandage had replaced his bloody shirt. They wrapped it several times around his chest and up over his left shoulder. In the area where his wound was, he could see the raised area that must be the gauze covering his wound. He was relieved to see the gauze and wrap were white and not red.

"So, I'm back in the hospital?" asked Quillon toward the woman.

"You're in the Foundations' clinic," replied the woman's voice. "They brought you here right after your episode yesterday."

Quillon relaxed and took a deep breath. He tightened back up again when something the woman said sunk in. "Yesterday! How long have I been asleep?"

"Relax," said the woman as she walked into his view. "You popped a few stitches, and they felt it would be best if they gave you something to keep you out for a while. My name is Doctor Alicia Taylor," she said. "We met briefly yesterday."

Quillon recognized her as the woman that had been with Georges when he had woken up from that terrible dream. He nodded and said, "I remember seeing you." He looked at his bandaged chest, then asked, "Am I going to be okay, Doctor?"

Taylor lifted her tablet. "Says here, there wasn't a lot of additional damage. They are worried that you will be slow to heal. It also says you may need to start wearing a sling again." Taylor lowered the tablet and said, "It's not my field, but sounds like it could have been worse. I can call a doctor if you want to speak to someone before we get started."

Quillon was a little confused. "You're not my doctor?"

"I've had some medical training, but my specialty is in psychology." She saw Quillon winch and added, "Parapsychology, to be exact."

"What did you say your name was?" asked Quillon. His head was clearing and knew he had heard that name before.

"Doctor Alicia Taylor."

"Of course," said Quillon, studying her. "You're the one Stephanus told me about. The one that wants to talk to my dead sister." Quillon chuckled and looked away from her. "I didn't understand him at the time, but I worried about it for several hours. Finally, I decided what he really said was you wanted to talk about my dead sister. That I've had lots of experience with."

"I wish he had said nothing to you about me," said Taylor, pulling over a chair. "It is important that we start this investigation with no preconceptions or biases. But it's true. I'm interested in the visits by your sister."

"So, what is it you want? Are you a medium or something?" asked Quillon, still not looking at Taylor. "It won't work, you know. I went to a few before, and nothing happened. Just like my doctor warned me. Turned out, it really was all in my head."

"And what do you believe now?" asked Taylor calmly. "Is your sister still in your head? Are those bandages imaginary too?"

Quillon glared at her for a second, then he relaxed and turned away and said, "Sorry."

"I know this is stressful, but we really have a lot to get done today," said Taylor.

Quillon put his hand on his head, checking to see if he had a temperature, hoping for an excuse to stay where he was. No luck. He rubbed his eyes and was getting ready to sit up when he noticed a bandage on his arm. "What's this?" he asked, nodding at his arm.

"I ordered a few tests,"

"When did this happen?" asked Quillon, touching the bandage.

"You were asleep, and I couldn't wait for you to wake up. Like I said, we are under a very short timeline to get results on this project."

Quillon struggled to a sitting position, fought back the pain, then quickly said, "I don't like what's happening here. This place is nothing but bad news. I've been attacked twice, been drugged, and now people are doing tests on me without my permission. I think it's time for me to go home."

"That's fine," said Taylor calmly, looking down at her tablet. "But you need to understand, if you leave now, you won't get an answer to what your sister wants. Plus, if things continue as they are, you will be dead in a few months. That's only a guess. Like I said, I'm not a doctor. I can get you a more accurate estimate."

Quillon sat staring at Taylor. He wasn't sure what surprised him more. Her wanting to help with his sister or her threats that he was going to die. He took a few seconds to check himself. He felt tired, but that has become the norm since the attack. Finally, he asked, "What do you mean, dead?"

"Dead, like in not alive," said Taylor. She smiled and placed her tablet on her lap.

"I know what dead means. Why are you saying I will be dead in a few months?"

"I'm looking at the result of your tests," Taylor said, tapping her tablet slightly. Doctor Demetrio is quite worried about your anemia. He believes you may also have an issue with your bone marrow. He said something is both slowing your production of blood cells, and, in his words, something is absorbing blood cells. She looked up to see if Quillon was following and was met with a blank stare.

Quillon put his hand over his chest and stared at Taylor. "Losing blood?" he mumbled. "Where? I'm not bleeding."

"In a way you are," said Taylor, tapping her chest.

Quillon paused for a second, then understanding showed on his face. "My rash?" he said, looking at the area around his wound. "What the...," he shouted. He had not noticed it a few seconds ago, but now he could see the red tendrils of his rash reaching out from the edges of his bandage like vines looking for sunlight. He could clearly see a pattern in lines that made up the rash, one that he found very familiar. "It's covering my entire chest," he said. "How did it get so big, so fast?"

"I believe your sister may have something to do with that," said Taylor.

"You believe me? That my sister is hurting me. I told her I was sorry, but she doesn't listen to me," said Quillon.

"Let's just say for now, it is clear you're suffering. I'm going to find out how and why. We also need to solve our real problem."

"You don't think this is a problem?" said Quillon, looking again at the markings on his chest.

"For you, yes. But it's your dreams that threaten everyone."

"I don't understand?" said Quillon.

"I'd rather wait until I've finished my investigation before I say more. Right now, you need to get dressed. I need you in my lab as soon as possible. I will send someone for you."

With that, Taylor stood and left.

Quillon sat on the edge of the bed, trying to take in what she had said.

What did she mean about my dreams threaten people? he thought. In the past, his dreams had focused on Henrietta's death. He came to understand it was his guilt that caused them. Post-Traumatic Stress, they had said. It took time, but he learned how to manage it. In his mind, this was much the same. These new dreams had something to do with the library where he was attacked. *Just More PTSD. I will learn to manage these just like I did in the past,* he thought.

Quillon looked back at his rash and touched it. There was no pain, but his skin was warm. *Henrietta, why are you doing this to me?* he thought as he shook his head. When he first started dreaming about Henrietta, shortly after her death, he had worried he was being haunted by her. That was before his therapist explained everything so well. Now things were different. Henrietta came to him while he was awake. The old thoughts about being haunted creeped back into his mind.

His dreams had been bad, but they were just dreams. They never hurt him, and he could not think of any way they could hurt anyone else. He studied the pattern on his chest. This was different, and according to Doctor Taylor, was putting his life in danger. *If this is real; Henrietta is real,* he thought.

Quillon looked around the small little room. There was only one other bed in the room and the desk where Taylor must have been sitting. It reminded him, in many ways, of the nurses' station at his college. The room was empty. The more he thought about Henrietta, the more tempted he was to call out to her. Finally, he got up the courage he needed and quietly called her name. He glanced around with mixed feelings, both hoping she would appear so he could confirm that she was real, and worried about what she would do if she appeared. He put his hand over his chest and said her name in a louder voice. Still nothing. He got up and just stood there, thinking about what to do next. He took a deep breath and shouted, "Henrietta, if you're here. Show yourself!"

Quillon did not move. He had shouted louder than he had planned. He almost shouted again when he heard someone say, "Anything?"

Quillon turned to find a thin middle-aged man, with shaggy shoulder-length brown hair and rounded gold colored wire-rimmed glasses, standing by the door. He was dressed in sneakers, dark cargo pants and a dark blue crewneck shirt with a rainbow stripe across it and the words 'Not the Doctor'.

Quillon shook his head at the question because he was afraid he might stammer if he answered. While he was not sure if Henrietta would answer, he had expected no one else to.

"Well, we are going to work on that as well. My name is Danny Jackson. I work with Doctor Taylor. She wanted me to take you back down to your room so you can get changed, then we'll join her in the lab. You up for it?"

Quillon nodded, grabbed a nearby bathrobe, and followed Jackson out the door. It surprised him how close they were to the elevator. Looking around, the hallway looked familiar. He must have walked right past the little clinic on the day of the party. He was sure this was the same elevator that he had used to get to his room. That meant the loading dock was just beyond a set of double doors in front of him.

He thought about how nice it would be to get some fresh air and felt the urge to just keep walking, but Jackson was in front of him, pointing to the elevator that had just arrived.

"That's strange," said Quillon, pointing to the floor selector buttons. Danny had tapped the panel with his card, but only the buttons for the First floor, B1 and B3, lit up.

"Oh, I guess they didn't tell you," said Jackson. "Only the levels you're allowed to visit will light up."

"I wonder what I have access to," said Quillon as the door opened on his floor.

"Be my guest," said Jackson, stepping back from the entrance.

Quilon tapped the panel with his card, but nothing happened. The only light that was lit was his floor.

"That sucks," said Jackson. "You should at least have access to B1. That's where my lab is."

"I need to get to the main floor too," said Quillon. He stepped out of the elevator while looking at his card.

"I'm sure it's a mistake," said Jackson. "Everyone needs to get to the main floor. The loading dock is the only place you can smoke here."

Quillon did not respond. A feeling of panic was growing in him as he looked around at his surroundings and back at the elevator.

"Don't worry. I will talk to my sister when we get to our lab. Alicia is great at pulling strings." said Jackson, putting his hand on Quillon's shoulder.

"Your sister?" asked Quillon. "Doctor Taylor is your sister?"

"Yeah. Younger sister," smiled Jackson. "Half-sister really. But don't tell her I told you. She doesn't like people knowing that she hired family."

Quillon just nodded and looked at his card again.

"Hey, we're here so, you go get changed and I will hang out with the guards for a while. Maybe even raid the mini fridge," said Jackson.

Quillon turned to walk towards his room, stopped, and said, "Just so you know, we don't go by the title guards any more. They are Security Officers."

"Good to know," said Jackson as he walked towards the cafeteria.

Quillon turned and headed for his room. *That's the first normal guy I met since I've been here,* he thought. *Hope his sister can get the elevator thing fixed. I would really like to see the sun again.*

Chapter 14
Good Old Jackson

Quillon showered and changed quicker than he had expected. He stood looking at the door to his apartment, trying to think of some reason to delay his meeting with Doctor Taylor. He was not afraid of her. It was just that the memories of his prior talks with psychologists were always so tiring. It seemed like they would take forever to get to something he wanted to talk about. Meeting after meeting, going over the same things. He knew little about parapsychology, but he was sure anything with the word psychology wouldn't be much different.

"Well, at least I'm getting paid for it this time," he said as he activated the door and stepped into the hallway.

He could hear laughing coming from the cafeteria at the end of the hallway. As he got to the window, he saw Jackson sitting on the edge of a table, drink in hand, surrounded by all three security officers on duty.

"What did you do next?" asked one officer.

Jackson spotted Quillon and waved. "I put a big rock on the cover and walked off. Leaving it for some other guy to deal with," he continued. The other officers all broke into laughs that quickly died out as they saw Quillon enter the room.

"It was fun guys, but work calls," said Jackson, standing. The officers, all of them smiling, said a quick goodbye and walked silently past Quillon.

Quillon wished he could just hang out with them and talk shop like Jackson, but Stephanus' no contact order, and the way they looked at him after his last little episode, made that impossible.

"All ready?" asked Jackson as he walked towards Quillon.

"Sounds like you were getting on okay with them," said Quillon.

"Just telling them some of the strange things I ran into during my time in the field," said Jackson as he headed toward the hallway.

"You know, I've never met a real ghost hunter before. How long have you been doing this?" asked Quillon, following behind.

"Since I was a small kid. I've spent more time in the field than my sister. In fact, I was the one that got her to come over to my side."

"Your side?" asked Quillon.

"I always believed in paranormal stuff. She is more into mind control, ESP, remote viewing, stuff like that," said Jackson as they stopped in front of the elevator. "Now that I'm working with her, we have reached an enjoyable working agreement. I find them and she bags them."

"Bags them?" asked Quillon as they stepped into the elevator.

Jackson tapped the elevator panel with his card and pressed the button for B1. "She does her best to disprove the existence of supernatural events. She will study them, and the people associated with them, until she understands why the event happened, or why people think it happened. She says there is value in studying both the real and the fake events, but someone has to have the courage to separate them first."

"So, she doesn't believe what is happening to me is true?" asked Quillon disappointedly.

"No," said Jackson. "She is positive something real is happening here. It's a pleasant surprise for me."

The elevator door opened on a floor that looked initially like the one he had just left, except for the absence of security. He saw four doors along both sides of the hallway. He also noticed a few potted plants placed sparingly around.

They stopped just a few doors to the right of the elevator and Jackson said, "Welcome to our lab," pointing toward the door. It was a plain dark wood door, with a dark blank nameplate held in a gold frame. Quillon noticed that the other doors all had name plates describing the users or purpose of the door. Even the broom closet had a name, but this one was blank.

"No nameplate?" asked Quillon.

"We move around a lot. Kind of gotten use to not having one," said Jackson as he opened the door. He paused before entering and said, "One word of warning, we don't use the title ghost hunters anymore. We like to be called Spectral Surveyors."

Quillon was ready to apologize for calling Jackson a ghost hunter when he saw the smile grow on Jackson's face. *Got me,* he thought, as he followed Jackson into the lab.

Chapter 15
Chocolate is Fine

At first glance, there was nothing very lab-like about the room. The left side resembled any normal office space, complete with two standard cubicles, cabinets, and a few basic bookcases. There were a few boxes in the back, still waiting to be unpacked.

It was on the right side where things got a little strange. It looked like something out of a movie set. In the back half of the room, sat what looked like a futuristic dentist chair. There was a rack hanging above it, with strange equipment and several cables hanging down. More cables came off the bottom of it and connected to a desk with several monitors. Next to the desk was a rack of computer hard drives.

The other half of the right side was taken up by a ten by eight-foot stage, equipped with a single chair and a small table. Nearby were a few microphones, lights, and a couple of cameras and recording and monitoring equipment.

"What's that?" Quillon asked, pointing toward the chair. "It looks like something from a horror movie."

"That's our sensory halo chair," said Jackson, walking over and placing his hand on it. "Special detection and monitor equipment, above and below it. The last place we worked in had an amazing one. It took up an entire room." Jackson looked back at the chair, tapped it again, and said, "Sadly, this is the best we can do in short order, but it should be okay for our time with you."

"Me?" said Quillon nervously. "What am I going to do with that?"

"Don't worry," said Jackson cheerfully. "I use something like this all the time. You sit in the chair. We wire you up to monitors." Jackson pointed to the rack above the chair. "It's a piece of cake. Nothing to worry about."

"What do we need that thing for?" asked Quillon. Still standing just inside the room. "I thought we were just going to talk."

"Sometimes it helps people recall things better," said Jackson. "Have you ever had a good idea just after you wake up but forget it shortly after?"

When Quillon nodded, Jackson continued, "That's because your mind gets busy handling all the information it's receiving and prioritizing what's available for your immediate use. That great idea is still there. It's just pushed down, packed in, with no hook to let you bring it back up. With this, we free your brain from all that distraction, leaving it free to do your bidding. It's a form of sensory deprivation. It lets you dig down deep and find those lost memories. Plus, if someone is tapping into your brain, we can spot it easier."

"Don't worry,"

Quillon jumped a few feet forward. Startled by the voice of Doctor Taylor coming from behind him.

"I'm sorry. I didn't mean to scare you," said Taylor apologetically. "Danny, get Quillon a chair."

"I'm okay," said Quillon as he took the small chair Jackson offered him. "Doctor Jackson was just showing me around."

Jackson tapped at the letters on his shirt and said, "You can call me Danny. Sis is the only doctor in the family."

"Danny, I asked you not to call me that in public," said Taylor. She looked irritated as she grabbed another chair and placed it a few feet from Quillon.

Quillon watched as Taylor seemed to compose herself again. Calmly she said, "Like I said, don't worry about the Halo Chair. We are going to talk first. If we feel it is necessary, we will explore, together, the use of the chair."

Quillon felt more at ease. He had never been to a session where they used something like that. He had been through hypnosis and some simple meditation techniques, but all of that had happened without climbing into a spaced-out dentist chair.

"Before we get to any of that," said Taylor, "I want you to know that we are going to go over details of your dreams and the visits by your sister. I know it's going to be uncomfortable, but take your time. Would you like something to drink? Maybe some milk and cookies?"

Quillon gave her a strange look but realize he was hungry. "I am a little hungry."

Taylor smiled, picked up the phone and told the person on the other end to bring some refreshment. She paused, then asked, "Is chocolate milk okay? I'm fond of it myself."

"Sure, that would be great," said Quillon, as he looked around at Jackson, who just smiled back at him.

"Chocolate is fine," Taylor said into the phone, then as she hung up, she stood and walked toward the little studio area. "Food will be here soon. I need you to have a seat over here. We are going to record your story. I also want to hook up some monitoring equipment. Nothing too uncomfortable. Something for monitoring brain waves and one of the little heart monitoring clips that go on your finger."

Quillon made himself as comfortable as he could. Jackson fitted him with a little headband with wires coming off it and put the heart monitoring clip on his finger. By the time the cookies and milk arrived, he was feeling much better about things.

"Okay, now what we want you to do is tell us about the dreams first," said Taylor. "We are going to ask you questions as you go along and may ask you to retell parts of it again. This isn't because we don't believe you, it is just that we have found people remember things during the retelling. Sometimes during the first interview, they leave things out they don't like or didn't think were important. Understand?"

When Quillon nodded, Taylor said, "Finish your milk and we'll get started." She reached for his glass once he was done and said, "Better?"

Surprisingly, Quillon felt much better. He took a breath and said, "I'm ready."

Taylor picked up the tray of snacks and said, "I have been told that I make some people nervous, so I'm going to leave now, but I'll be nearby, if needed." She looked at Jackson and said, "Stick to the dreams! Understand Danny?"

"I understand, but you're going to let me investigate it later, right? You promised."

"The link is our number one priority. Your project can wait," said Taylor sternly.

Quillon felt like he was watching a kid being told he could not stay up late to see a movie. As he was explaining what he dreamed, Quillon could sense Jackson wanting to ask more questions. The ones he asked were really strange, like did he hear any buzzing noise or did he smell or taste anything during the dream. Quillon told him about smelling the blood and the feeling of being hungry. The uncontrollable feeling of anger. He really got Jackson's attention when he talked about feeling he was in another world, just on the other side. How cold it was and what it looked like. He ended up mixing in a little from the other dreams where he had similar experiences.

Taylor was right about the questioning, bringing back things he had forgotten. It surprised him how easy it was to talk to Jackson. He was honestly interested in what Quillon had to say. Quillon must have talked for at least three hours, all of it about his dreams and nothing really about Henrietta. They stopped for a break when a tray of ice cream arrived.

"Another gift from my sister," said Jackson, handing Quillon a bowl. As he took a scoop, Jackson said, "Sometimes she tries things like scented candles, or we might play cards first. I never know what she is going to do or why."

"I don't mind," said Quillon, enjoying his ice cream. "I wonder how she knew what I liked?"

"She is really thorough about her work, but not good with other things," said Jackson, finishing his bowl. "I'm always reminding her about birthdays and such." He stretched and said, "Ready to get back to work?"

"How am I doing?" asked Quillon, tapping on the wires attached to his headband.

"Surprisingly well," said Jackson. "Some of the stuff you said even freaked me out."

"I know," said Quillon. "I'm not new to nightmares, so that makes it a little easier for me." He paused for a second to finish his ice cream, then setting the bowl aside he said, "I was wondering when we get to talk about Henrietta? That's what I'm most worried about."

"We'll get to her," said Jackson. "It's important to learn more about your dreams so we can understand what triggers them and the link between them and your sister."

When Jackson saw the confusion on Quillon's face, he said, "You told us your sister never shows up before a dream starts."

"That's right," said Quillon.

"So, we are wondering, how does she know you're having a dream?"

"I think I understand," said Quillon. "Stop the dreams, and I can stop Henrietta. That's great."

"Yes and no," said Jackson. "We also need to explore the fact that she appears both in and after your dream. In fact, I think you said sometimes you felt she impacted your dreams, even ending them, after which she hurt you."

Quillon touched his chest, then said, "Yes." Still rubbing his chest, he continued, "This tattoo is her fault. I don't know why, but the more real the dream feels, the more she hurts me."

"Yes, the tattoo," said Jackson, glancing at the readouts. "I can see this upsets you more than talking about the dreams."

"Of course," said Quillon, "The dreams, while uncomfortable and creepy, never hurt. Henrietta does."

"Tell me," said Jackson, "After everything we talked about today, are you sure that those dreams are just dreams?"

Quillon started to answer, but paused to think about the question. Before he could respond, the phone rang. He watched as Jackson attempted to talk with the person on the other end. He could hear a woman's voice in between Jackson's broken attempt to apologize.

When the call ended, Jackson stood looking at the phone in his hand for several seconds, then glanced up at a camera mounted nearby. He gently hung up the phone, turned back to Quillon and, with a narrow smile, said, "My sister is going to join us soon. She wants to be the one to talk to you about your sister."

Quillon knew enough to tell that Jackson's kid sister had just chewed him out. *What had gotten her so upset?* he thought. It made Jackson's last question rest uneasy in his mind. He had always felt the dreams were too real. He had even said that several times. Now memories of those words came back to him, forcing him to think hard about what he had been telling others all along.

Chapter 16
Attack from Mars

Quillon laid in his bed, dressed, restlessly reviewing the events of yesterday. Doctor Taylor's return to the lab was, to say the least, uncomfortable. The tension between Taylor and Jackson was thick enough to cut with a knife, and Quillon was becoming uncomfortable with her insistence on talking about his dreams. She had avoided any discussion about Jackson's last questions by switching to a discussion of the events surrounding Henrietta's death.

It was just like his old sessions. The same old questions, like 'Why do you blame yourself?' and 'Why do you think she wants to hurt you?', to which, he gave his same old answers. He explained how he was babysitting and too busy playing a video game to watch her. When she kept pestering him to play with her, he sent her to go get a book. Next thing he knew, the bookcase fell, and she was screaming for him to help her. He couldn't lift the bookcase, so he ran to the neighbors. When they got back, her screaming had stopped. They wouldn't let him back in and the next time he saw her was at the funeral.

After that, Quillon got more emotional as Taylor probed for similarities and differences between Henrietta in his dreams and now. At one point it was too much, and Quillon broke down in tears. The meeting ended with Jackson's welcome suggestion to call it quits for the day, and Taylor's agreement to look into the security settings on Quillon's elevator pass.

Quillon had tossed and turned last night and had gotten very little sleep. The night had been full of dreams. Thankfully, none of them were about the library or Henrietta. He remembered in one being trapped in the elevator yelling for help. In the other, he had found himself the only person on his floor. No guards anywhere and surprisingly, that had scared him. A few times he had thought about peeking out to see if anyone was still out there.

It bothered Quillon that there wasn't a clock in the room. So, when he woke up the last time, he got up, showered, dressed and laid back down, waiting for his morning wake up call. Time crawled. There was nothing to do except lay there thinking about the wake up call. Just when he was ready to scream from boredom, the little LED flashed. "Finally!" he shouted.

As Quillon passed the elevator on the way to the cafeteria, he was tempted to check his pass card. He felt bad about threatening to leave if they did not fix it by the morning, but he could not think of any reason for him not being able to get to the main floor. He wasn't a prisoner, after all.

Quillon tried greeting the security officer sitting at the back of his little room. The greeting was not returned. *Guess I'm still off limits*, he thought as he continued towards the cafeteria. A strange dinging sound coming from the recreation room caught Quillon's attention. He peeked inside and saw Jackson in the back corner playing an 'Attack from Mars' pinball machine.

When Jackson saw him, he gave a quick wave, and shouted, "Go eat! I'll join you in a few."

Quillon hadn't explored the recreation room. Stephanus said it was full of games he would enjoy. He had never really liked pinball, but he had collected the 'Mars Attacks' trading cards. He made a note to check it out later.

The cafeteria was empty, but there was food on the line. In a way, he was glad. It made it that much easier to enjoy his food without dealing with the cold shoulder from the other officers. The emptiness was strange. He had only seen one officer this morning. He wondered where the other two officers were. The concern quickly left him as he finished his food. He was getting up for another glass of juice when Jackson entered.

"That was fun. I haven't played pinball for years," said Jackson, as he joined Quillon for a drink. "I didn't even know they still made them. And some of those old arcade games, man, you really got it made here."

"I'm glad you like it, but I'm getting a little tired of being here. You guys said you could fix what's going on before it killed me," said Quillon.

"That's the plan," said Jackson. "Believe it or not, we learned a lot yesterday. Like I told you before, part of what we do is disproving things. Like old Sherlock said, what's left over is what you want, or something like that."

"What have you disproved?" asked Quillon, pushing his tray aside.

"Well, we don't think you're crazy," said Jackson as he took a seat across from Quillon. "We also believe that you're not in control of when your dreams begin or stop."

"I knew that before we started," Quillon said disappointedly. "Tell me something new."

"You are suffering physical trauma from both your dreams and your sister's visit," said Jackson, playing with the cup in front of him.

Tapping his chest, Quillon said, "I know about the tattoo, but I don't understand how my dreams are hurting me." He paused for a second, then continued, "or others, according to your sister."

Jackson took a sip, thought for a while as if trying to decide how to continue, then said, "The piece of dagger in your chest is doing something with your blood. At first, we thought it was working something like bone cancer, preventing you from producing blood cells."

Quillon nodded. He had heard Doctor D talk about testing for cancer. He hoped Jackson wasn't getting ready to confirm that fear. "I know they were concerned about the possibility of cancer or heart failure."

Jackson looked around the room. No effort had been taken to hide the camera that was monitoring the area. Jackson leaned closer to Quillon and said in a low voice, "I believe that the fragment in your chest is absorbing blood." He looked around again and continued, "That's what triggers both your chest pains and your dreams."

Quillon just stared at Jackson, who sat back and put a finger to his lips. As strange as it seemed, Jackson's suggestion kind of made sense. Looking around, it sunk in for maybe the first time that he was in the basement of an organization that believed in magic. He had accepted help from Jackson and Taylor because they had talked about things like ESP and ghosts. He could accept those. Henrietta was proof that he was dealing with something unnatural. But magic? That was something that he had resisted. "Your sister believes this, too?"

"Let's keep this between you and me for now," said Jackson, looking back at the camera.

"You're talking about magic," said Quillon, leaning forward. "What does that have to do with Henrietta?"

"Let's just forget I said anything for now," said Jackson, looking at his watch. As he stood, he said, "Time to go. Sis will be waiting. We're going to spend the day figuring out who or what Henrietta is, and why she is hurting you."

Quillon knew who Henrietta was. He could also understand why she might want to hurt him. But he had no idea what she had to do with his dreams or the tattoo. "I think you're wrong about magic," said Quillon. "Henrietta is real. She is a ghost. Not a zombie or the results of some voodoo magic."

"Your probably right," said Jackson as they walked toward the elevator. "Just because this place studies magic doesn't mean that someone is using it on you."

Quillon stopped for a second and watched Jackson continue to the elevator door.

Jackson looked back and said, "Come on. This will give you a chance to check out the access on your card."

Quillon joined Jackson, card in hand. He let the hope of seeing that first floor button light push the talk of magic deep down in his mind, where he could forget it for now.

Chapter 17
Time in the Chair

Quillon's trip to the first floor gave him two new bits of information. First, he learned where the other two officers were. They had been posted just outside the elevator door on the first floor, and looked none too happy to see him. Second, now that he could reach the first floor, he didn't have a real urge to go outside. It was a relief to see the first floor button light up, but the B1 button just brought back into focus why he was there. When Jackson asked if he wanted to step outside for a second. He said, "No, your sister and mine are waiting. Let's get this over with."

It surprised both Jackson and Quillon to find the lab empty and the lights out.

"Hum, that's strange," said Jackson looking at his watch. "She should be here already."

"So, what's that mean?" asked Quillon, following Jackson inside. "Are we going to reschedule our meeting?"

"No," said Jackson as he flipped on the rest of the lights and headed toward the Halo Chair. "I'm sure she got delayed talking to some big shot. She's not much of a talker, but when she does, she can really talk." Jackson headed to the desk near the chair and turned on a few switches. "This is good. It'll give us some time to get you ready for your ride."

Quillon reluctantly followed Jackson toward the Halo Chair but stopped when he noticed the fresh addition to the room. It was a large photo mural that covered about twelve feet of the wall behind the Halo Chair. It was a photo of a dirt path that ran through a thick green forest and disappeared into the distance. The light shown though the green of the trees, giving a warm comfortable feeling. Along the sides of the path, peaking out of overgrown flowering brushes, were rows of stone that looked at first like a kind of discarded fence. "That's nice," said Quillon, until he looked a little closer and said, "Is that a graveyard?"

"Yes," said Jackson, taking a second to admire the photo. "I had it put up last night. It's one of my favorites."

"But it's a graveyard," said Quillon, still staring at the wall.

Jackson smiled, then said, "When I was in high school, there was a graveyard across the street. I would sit in my boring English class and just study it, wondering about the people buried there. It's what got me into this kind of work."

"It is pretty, if you can get past the dead people," said Quillon.

"I took this picture myself. I have an entire collection of famous graveyards. I try to visit a few every year." Jackson paused for a few seconds, then when he turned round, he said, "Helps me keep my head on straight." Turning back to the photo, Jackson said, "I'm sure you do the same thing. Keep little things nearby that remind you why you're doing what you do."

Quillon thought about that and realized he had nothing. He only did what he did because someone had told him he needed to do something. Glenn's offer of full-time work was the first that had come along.

"I see you got your picture up," said Taylor as she entered the lab. "I was hoping you were going to put up the one from India with the ocean view."

Quillon turned to greet Taylor, but what came out was, "That's the puzzle box. The one from the library."

Taylor was standing in the doorway with the box held in her arms. "You're right," she said, walking to a nearby table and putting it down. "I just came from a meeting where it was suggested that I put more effort into learning how it's linked to you and your sister."

Both Quillon and Jackson walked over to the table where the box was sitting. "Professor Georges wanted me to close it again," said Quillon as he picked up the box. "Yep. It's still open," said Quillon. Moments later, the room spun and went dark.

Chapter 18
Puppet Master

The moonless sky and men dressed in brown cloaks, each carrying torches, told Quillon he was not in the library. He felt a chill in the air, and without thinking, he pulled the cloak tighter and held the torch closer to enjoy its warmth. Looking down, he saw he was standing in a small circle. The other torchbearers had their own. These circles orbited the outer edge of another large circle. Inside this larger circle was a man dressed in a dark cloak with gold and red trim, two low platforms, like benches, and a stone pedestal.

A horrible sound, like the whining of a wounded animal, filled the air. Quillon couldn't see the source of the sound. He guessed it came from deep within a dark thick forest that met a line of high hedges marking the edge of a clearing, twenty or thirty feet behind the man directly across from him.

Movement to his right caught his attention. When he looked, he saw a young, tall, thin woman with blond hair, dressed in a full-length white cloth gown, much like a thick nightgown. There was something familiar about her. He found he could not look away. As he watched her, she smiled, and his eyesight blurred. When his vision cleared, Henrietta stood in her place, dressed in her burial dress. She smiled at him again, but this time like she was amused. His eyes told him it was Henrietta, but she looked different now. Almost alive. He could see the wind blowing the hem of her gown.

Quillon could only watch as Henrietta walked over to one of the platforms. Another woman took her place at the other, escorted by a cloaked man carrying several items which he placed on the stone pedestal.

Quillon tried to call to her but couldn't. He saw Henrietta raise a finger to her lips, as if telling him to be quiet. She then pointed her finger toward the forest, which seemed to respond to her gesture with another loud and terrifying scream.

Quillon glanced in the direction she pointed, and this time he heard movement. The darkness still cloaked the details of the movement, but he could hear crashing trees and thought he saw a movement of the closest branches.

Quillon could tell that the man dressed in the red and gold cloak was the leader of the group. He watched as the leader raised his hand and both Henrietta and the other woman laid down on the platforms. Next, the leader picked up items from the nearby pedestal and placed one on Henrietta and another on the other woman.

When the man stepped back, Quillon could see that a plain grey box sat on Henrietta's chest. The item on the other woman caused his stomach and chest to cramp so badly he thought he was going to puke. It was the dagger, identical to the one he had been stabbed with. Quillon looked back at Henrietta. The box on her chest was the same size as his, but there was not that crazy pattern on it.

The men in the surrounding circles started chanting. Quillon realized he was watching some crazy ritual like in the late movies; where people like this summoned a demon and were all killed. Quillon wanted to yell for it to stop, but no matter how hard he tried, no words came out.

He looked at the other torchbearers for help, but saw most of their faces locked, wide eyed in an expression of horror. He followed their stares to the forest and saw several sets of tentacles reaching through the hedge, with the glint of a pair of enormous eyes in a dark mass behind them.

The torchbearers held their place as the tentacles slowly made their way toward them. Quillon heard another horrifying scream, but this one came from the direction of Henrietta and the other woman. He looked back in time to see the leader plunge the dagger into the spot where it had laid on the woman's chest.

There was a loud roar from the darkness, and the tentacles stopped their advance. In the clearing, Quillon saw a swirling mass floating in the air. He heard a last cry from the stabbed woman and saw the mass grow into a portal at least twenty feet high. He then understood that the dagger, the portal, and the creature in the darkness were all from his dream.

Quillon turned back to Henrietta, praying that nothing had happened to her. The leader stood before her and took a red glowing item, like an amulet, from round his neck and placed it on the box sitting on Henrietta's chest. As soon as the amulet touched the box, Henrietta started to spasm. The leader held the amulet to the box and pressed down on it and Quillon thought he saw it sinking into her chest. Henrietta's whole body glowed white hot, and the box glowed red.

The leader stepped back, and Quillon could see the box pulling the light from Henrietta's small, shaking body. As it did, the box glowed brighter and brighter, pulsing in a red pattern that Quillon recognized. The leader stepped forward and picked up the box. As he did, Henrietta's body seemed to deflate until all that was left was the barely recognizable shape of a body that could not even provide shape to the clothes that covered it.

The cries of the creature and the roar of the portal couldn't draw Quillon's attention from the body of Henrietta. He had struggled to live through her death once before. Seeing her die again took away all his worry for his own safety. The leader walked back to the center of the circle, carrying the box that had taken Henrietta's life.

Quillon wanted to look away but felt as if he was being forced to watch as the leader pulled out a shiny thin item, like a needle, and stuck in into his hand. Next, he placed his hand on the box and slumped forward. A few minutes passed and nothing happened. The creature stayed where it was. The portal churned, and the leader stayed slumped. Then, with a jerk, he stood up straight.

The leader began making strange movements, almost like a puppet on a string. Quillon heard the creature roar and felt himself being forced to look at it. His dreams gave him no idea of what the creature looked like. Now, as it moved into the clearing, he got his first real look.

The thing was hideous! Obviously, not of this world. Its shape reminded Quillon of a cross between a centipede and a squid. It had several small, short legs coming out of a torso of overlapping bands. The first two bands nearest the front had eight large tentacles each. Its head section, which was raised up, as if the creature was a cobra ready to strike, resembled a squid, with a hard skull-like face that extended out and above a gapping mouth that was surrounded by several smaller tentacles, of different lengths, that reached out in all direction like feelers. The body ended in a flat, heavy spade shaped tail that swept back and forth providing support for the creature's raised head as it turned from side to side.

The creature moved forward in jerky movements, almost like it was being dragged. Quillon looked back at the leader to see him mimic walking. He looked like a puppet on a string. Slowly Quillon understood the leader was causing the creature to move forward. He thought back to when he had felt like he had control of the creature in his dreams.

The creature slowly advanced toward the small group and the portal. Quillon could see the leader struggling with controlling the tentacles, keeping them from reaching out to the torchbearer. *Why is he bringing it this way?* he thought. He soon understood the leader was moving the thing toward the portal. It looked like the closer it got to the portal, the stronger the pull it appeared to have on the creature. Soon, its enormous body was being sucked into the portal.

When the last of the thing's body was through, the leader quickly retrieved the dagger from the chest of the woman, where it was resting, and put it into the box. He closed the lid, and the portal closed as well with a snap and a last-minute hiss of wind.

With that, the darkness closed in on Quillon until all that was left was a table with the box on it. His hand resting on top of it. Quillon looked up and saw Henrietta standing only a few feet from him. She took a step forward, and he felt her place her hand on his. He felt a chill, then a burning and itching that was soon followed by darkness.

When he opened his eyes, he was looking up at Jackson and Taylor. His head hurt and he itched all over.

"Are you okay?" asked Jackson, offering his hand to help Quillon up.

"I think so," said Quillon, getting to his feet. He looked around for Henrietta but did not see her. "Where is she? Did you see her?" he asked, still looking around.

"See who?" asked Taylor.

"Henrietta," said Quillon. "She was just here."

"We saw nothing," said Jackson. "But maybe the equipment did. I had it running, getting ready for you to use the chair."

"What happened to you?" asked Taylor. "As soon as you touched the box, you spaced out, then a few seconds later you fell to the ground shaking."

"A few seconds? That can't be right," said Quillon. "My dream lasted a lot longer than that."

"More dreams about the library?" asked Jackson from across the room.

"No," said Quillon as he sat down in a chair. "I think this was more a history lesson from Henrietta about the box, the dagger, the creature, and the portal."

"I'm going to need you to sit in that chair by the recording equipment," said Taylor. "I want you to tell me everything you can remember."

Quillon nodded and as he walked over to the studio area, Jackson said, "Well, your sister was here. That's for sure."

"Did you get any readings?" asked Taylor.

"No, but I can see that his tattoo has grown. It's now peeking out of his shirt sleeves and collar."

Quillon glanced at his shirt sleeve, then pulled his collar out enough to look down at his chest. It was covered from his waist to his neck. He thought back to his dream, remembered how Henrietta's body had been absorbed into the box. It upset him thinking about it, but as he stared at the tattoo, a thought came to him and he said, "Maybe this is just one way for me to get closer to you, Henrietta."

Chapter 19
I Don't Do Weird

Georges leaned back in his chair and rubbed his eyes. He had just spent most of the morning reading over the comments from Doctor Taylor on her discussion with Quillon about his dream about the Necro Box. The thickness of the folder did nothing to hide the gravity of what it contained. He would need to be very careful about how he proceeded.

There was a rap on his office door that caught Georges off guard. Normally, his assistant would announce all visitors. Georges closed the folder and shouted, "Come in!"

"Greetings, Ian," said Yuri as he entered, a large smile resting below his shaded aviator glasses. "I hope you don't mind that I let myself in. Your man was away from his desk, and I could not figure out how to ring you, so I knocked."

Glad for the interruption, Georges stood and took a few steps toward the door, stopping at the closest padded chair. He patted it and said, "Have a seat, Yuri. We have a lot to discuss today."

"Am I late?" he asked as he looked around. "Where are the others?"

"No, you're on time," said Georges, shaking Yuri's hand before heading back to his desk. He recovered two glasses from the cabinet and pulled a bottle from the desk drawer. He held it up for Yuri, who nodded. While he was pouring the drinks, he said, "Stephanus is handling the arrival of the other Regents."

"I should have guessed," said Yuri. "I bumped into Torry Wellington this morning. I haven't seen him in person since the last formal regent meeting. What was that, eight years ago?"

"Twelve," said Georges, as he returned to his desk. "Reggie Ashwind is at the airport and will be here soon."

"Torry, Reggie, Jordan, you, and me," said Yuri, counting each name on his fingers. "That makes five of thirteen. Anyone else coming?"

"Not sure. I did my best to remind them of the importance of their positions and the proximity of an uncontrolled creature, summoned from who knows where. I'm pretty sure that Markham and Tatsuya will show up. Not sure if that's a good thing, since they are both supporters of Elliott. The three of them together, has always ended up in a rehash over leadership."

"Well, you still got my vote," said Yuri, accepting the drink Georges handed him. Looking around, Yuri said, "Something's different about your office." Yuri pointed to the half columns in each of the corners, each with a large, dark chunk of stone on them. "Those are new. Are they Black Tourmaline Logs?"

"Yes," said Georges, with a bit of pride.

"I don't think I have seen specimens that large before," said Yuri.

"I got them on-line, from a site called Natural Collective. My pride is the large Kyanite crystal cluster above the door."

"Very nice. I don't remember you having that strong an interest in that area of our work."

"I had lunch the other day with Mike and Mary Whitcomb from our Metaphysical department. They suggested those," Georges paused and pulled a yellow stone from his pocket, "and citrine. As you can guess, I have been under a little stress lately, but I could not shake the feeling that something more was going on. I was worried that someone was acting against me."

Yuri smiled and said, "Like hexes?"

"Don't forget what we do here," said Georges in a more serious tone as he returned to his desk. He poured himself another drink. "Refill?" he asked, motioning toward Yuri with the bottle.

"No, I'm fine, thanks," said Yuri, setting his glass on the nearby table. "Need to be clearheaded when Taylor gets here. She is very quick-witted and has a way of getting the better of you in a conversation if you're not ready."

Georges picked up Taylor's report and held it out for Yuri, who took it and sat back down.

"That's Doctor Taylor's final report," said Georges, taking another sip.

"Final report?" said Yuri as he opened the folder.

"Doctor Taylor has decided, in her words, 'This project no longer fits the criteria for our participation.' She and her brother are packing and should be gone before the end of the day."

"What? You're kidding," said Yuri, "What happened? Did she have another run in with Elliott?"

"No, nothing that simple," said Georges. He leaned back in his chair, looking across the room at the monitor with its never-ending display of the portal, and said, "She gave her reasons in the report. Quillon had another dream. A very different one this time. Doctor Taylor believes the dream was orchestrated by an entity acting as his dead sister in an effort to give the genuine history of the Necro Box and its relationship to the creature."

"That's great. We are going to have something in time for the regent meeting." said Yuri, paging through the report. "It sure is thorough. Can you just summarize her conclusions for me?"

"She said the root of everything that is happening with Quillon is magic," said Georges, playing with his glass. "Her report says even what looks like paranormal activity results from magic. She finds that both unnatural and weird. She made it clear that she didn't do weird because it was unprofessional and too dangerous."

"Doesn't do weird," said Yuri, almost to himself. "She deals with the dead. That's pretty weird."

"That was my comment, but I can assure you she was scared," said Georges. "Quillon's dream suggested the Necro Box contains the soul of a sacrificed woman. They used it to control the movements of the creature, forcing it to enter the portal, which, in fact, is really a prison of some kind."

"You're saying we unlocked the prison, and the thing is trying to escape?" asked Yuri, as he joined Georges in watching the churning portal.

Neither man said anything for a few minutes until Yuri said, "That brings us back to our original problem of keeping it from getting out. We are no better off now than when we started."

"Actually, we have learned a lot," said Georges, and I must compliment Doctor Taylor on how she could put the pieces together. I doubt Elliot could have provided better insight into our problem. He can only view the problem one way and, according to Taylor, he has made a few major erroneous assumptions.

"What are those?" asked Yuri, putting the folder back on Georges' desk.

"First, the dagger is linked to the portal and not the creature. Its purpose for being summoned, though a blood sacrifice, is to open so the creature can be driven through it."

"Now that we have summoned again it, it just wants to open wide, like a doorway," said Yuri. "It must not care what side the creature is on. That means Elliott was wrong about the portal acting like a summoning circle for the creature."

"Correct. We still do not know why or how the creature was summoned. That means there is no way to complete, or act on, the creature's summoning spell," said Georges.

"And the other thing we learned?" asked Yuri.

Georges paused for a second. "The Necro Box is acting on its own to achieve the purpose they designed it for, which is, keep the prison door locked."

"Acting on its own. That's the part that upset Taylor, right?"

"I don't agree that magic was used to infuse the Necro Box with the soul of a person," said Georges. "There are lots of examples where inanimate object act on instructions. Take Golems for example."

"If its job is to lock the prison door, why hasn't it done so?" asked Yuri, again looking at the monitor.

"In the dream, the portal closed once someone locked away the dagger inside the Necro Box." Georges got up and retrieved the box from the safe. He studied it for a few seconds, then as he placed it on his desk said, "If true, it won't close because all the pieces are not inside."

"It appears Elliot was wrong about a lot," said Yuri, sitting back in his chair. "Killing Quillon with the dagger won't complete the summoning, and it won't close the portal."

"It's Taylor's belief that locking the dagger inside the box somehow breaks the link between the dagger and the portal," said Georges. "If that is true, it conflicts with my prior belief that cutting off the blood supply was what closed the portal. I'm honestly not sure which is true."

"I can't wait to see the look on Elliott's face when you tell him this," said Yuri, smiling. "You're going to spring it on him during the meeting, right?"

Georges said nothing. He picked up both the Necro Box and the report and placed them in his safe. Closing it, he sat down and studied Yuri for a few minutes before saying, "You're one of my oldest and dearest friends here. I have always counted on your trust in my judgement."

Yuri smiled nervously and said, "I appreciate that. But, I also know when you're going to pull some stunt that is going to get me in hot water later. What are you planning?"

Georges said nothing but returned to playing with his glass.

"You're not going to give that report to the other Regents, are you?" said Yuri cautiously.

"Not right away," said Georges. "I intend on giving it after the meeting. Once I have had more time to evaluate it."

"Once the other Regents learn that Doctor Taylor has abandoned the project, they will have no choice but to give it to Elliott."

"I'm counting on that," said Georges.

Yuri sat quietly in his chair, studying Georges. "What are you up to?"

"The Regents will order me to give Elliott access to the Quillon, but they would never take control of the project from me," said Georges. "I would simply allow him to carry out his experiments, while I did mine."

"You know he will probably kill Quillon in order to close the portal," said Yuri.

"That is a possibility," said Georges. "To tell you the truth, I'm not sure if Doctor Taylor's assumptions about the box are correct. If Quillon were to die, the worst thing that could happen would be that the portal would not get any larger. Who knows, it might even close."

"That's taking a big chance," said Yuri. "I thought you would have wanted to explore Taylor's theory."

Georges leaned towards Yuri. In a voice that did not hide his excitement, said, "I feel that the real power, the one that will put us back on the top is the magic of the Necro Box," said Georges. "Imagine, being able to create an object that acts intelligently, almost like Artificial Intelligence. The possibilities are almost unimaginable." Georges leaned back, glanced at the monitor, and said, "Elliott can have his creature. I want the box!"

Chapter 20
Visit to a Graveyard

Quillon was up hours before his wake-up call. It had been a restless night, with bits of his vision yesterday flashing through his sleep. He had taken a shower, dressed and was lying on his bed trying to relax, but that was useless. He wished he had something to focus on, a radio, a book, his cell phone, anything to get his mind off yesterday.

"The arcade," he said, sitting up. He had wanted to check out the game Jackson had been playing the other day. *Maybe I can beat his high score,* he thought happily.

When he left his room, it surprised him to see only half of the overhead fixtures were on. Quillon stopped at the little room for security and found an officer sitting with his back to the little half door, feet propped up on another chair and a book lying open on his lap. Quillon made a sound like he was clearing his throat.

Without moving, the officer said, "You're up early." He turned around slowly, glanced at his watch and said, "Food will not be ready for at least another hour."

"No problem. I'm going to spend some time on the games," said Quillon, pointing towards the recreation room.

The officer nodded, got up and flicked a switch in a cluster on the wall, and the light in the recreation room came on.

"Thanks," said Quillon. Just before he headed towards the games, he said, "Can you let me know when the food is ready?"

"You'll know," said the officer as he returned to his seat and picked up his book.

The last site Quillon had been working before the attack was a night shift. He could relate to the officer's boredom, especially with no entertainment available. *I wonder why he didn't just jump on the games for a few hours,* he thought. His question was answered when he noticed that all the games had a card reader installed where the coin slot would have been.

There were three arcade style video games, three pinball machines, and what looked like a video poker machine. Quillon had heard of the three video games, but had never actually seen or played them. *These games are almost as old as me,* he thought as he walked past them. The pinball machines were colorful and interesting. Quillon had played a pinball game on his phone, but never the real thing. He made his way to the Attack from Mars machine and studied it for a few minutes. He was not sure what to do, but he had an hour or so to learn. Quillon tapped his card. The machine responded, and he soon got lost in the noise and excitement of the game.

Quillon wasn't sure how long he had been playing when the lights turning on in the hallway caught his attention. *Must be time to eat,* he thought. He shook his hands in front of him, surprised how sore they felt.

He finished up the last round, disappointed to see that he hadn't beaten Jackson's high game. *Not that bad for a first time,* he thought as he glanced over toward the window. He saw a security officer head for the cafeteria. *Wonder if I'm still off limits,* he thought. *I don't want to sit with someone who's going to ignore me the whole time.* Quillon looked back at the game and thought, *One more game. Then I'll go eat.*

He was halfway through his second game when Morgan stuck his head in and said, "Last call on the food."

Quillon thanked him and said he would be right in as soon as he finished.

Morgan said, "You may not have that much time, it's shift change. Also, there is a package for you. They should've given it to you earlier."

Quillon watched as the next two balls when down the drain. "A package? From whom?"

"It didn't say. You can pick it up at the booth," said Morgan, who headed for the cafeteria.

Quillon took a breath, stepped back from the machine. "A package?" he murmured. *Maybe it's the refill on my pills,* he thought. *I'm getting low. I was wondering how I went about reordering some.*

As he walked past the cafeteria toward the security station, he saw Morgan was right. It was getting crowded. There were already four officers in line for food. *Hope I have enough time to eat before Jackson shows up,* he thought.

As soon as he had the package in his hands, he knew it was not his pills. It was one of those large, padded cellophane envelopes, and it was heavy.

Quillon made his way back to the cafeteria, put his package on the table, and got his food. As he sat down, he could see that it had the interest of the others sitting around him. Quillon picked at his food, studying the package. There was no label. No sender's information. Just his first name written in cursive with a fat blue felt pen.

Soon, the only ones left in the cafeteria were Quillon and Morgan. Quillon pushed his tray aside and moved the package in front of him. He ran his finger over it, and he could feel something inside, like a binder. He looked back at Morgan, who said, "I got nowhere to be right now. Thought I would enjoy my coffee a little longer."

Quillon realized Morgan wasn't going to leave. He could either go back to his room or open it here. "Might as well get it over with," he said as he attempted to open the envelope. After a few seconds of struggling with the flap, Morgan took out a knife and said, "Let me help you."

Seconds later, the envelope was open, and the contents were on the table. "It's a photo album," said Quillon as he flipped through it.

"Are those graveyards?" asked Morgan.

"Yeah, Jackson collected pictures of them," said Quillon, as he continued to study the pages. There were four photos to a page, each in a little pocket, like the kind he had seen used to hold collectable cards. At the back of the album, he found a folded piece of paper. It was a note from Jackson. He read it several times, trying to understand it. Quillon saw Morgan studying him, so he said, "Jackson and his sister are done here. They are heading off to another assignment. He left this as a goodbye gift." There was more, but he didn't want to share it.

"Hum," said Morgan, as he stood up and finished his coffee. When he saw the confused look on Quillon's face, he said, "People come and go here all the time," said Morgan. "You get used to it after a while."

"I was supposed to have a meeting with them today," said Quillon. "I wonder what happens now?"

"I didn't see anyone on your schedule for today," said Morgan. "Guess you got the day off. More time to play those games."

Quillon watched as Morgan left, leaving him alone with his photo album and Jackson's note. He read it again, several times, especially the part that said his sister didn't think there was anything they could do about his situation since they only work with the paranormal, not the magical. The last paragraph said he should take time to enjoy the picture of the graveyard in India, the one near the ocean. A visit to it would be very enlightening. There was a second PostScript that said, 'Don't forget your camera.'

Quillon remembered how nervous Jackson was the last time they had talked in the cafeteria. Looking up, he noticed the camera. He was so used to seeing them in his line of work that he almost forgot about them. He noticed more when there wasn't one around.

He decided to take the package back to his room, where he hadn't discovered a camera. Quillon checked the envelope one more time as he walked back to his room, but found nothing else. Once there, he tossed the binder on the table near the bed. He laid down and read the note again.

What did he mean by not paranormal? he thought. *Henrietta is a ghost. I thought we all agreed on that.* He laid there a few minutes more, just staring at the letter. *I can't believe they would just take off like that, and what made him think I wanted a collection of graveyard pictures?*

Quillon sighed, then sat up. He picked up the photo and flipped through the pages. It wasn't hard to find the picture Jackson had referenced in the letter because there was a gold star sticker on it, like kids got in kindergarten. He looked at it for a few seconds and had to admit it was a pleasant view. He was getting ready to toss the album back on the table when he noticed there was something behind that photo. Quillon pulled the photo out and found sheets of toilet paper neatly folded and tucked into the plastic pocket. He could see that there was writing on it. He read it several times despite the chill the words gave him. The messages said, "Sis quit. Too dangerous. Dreams are real. Trust your sister. Flush this. Tell no one."

Quillon looked around nervously. Crumpled the note and flushed it as instructed. The lack of doors made him anxious. He suddenly felt like he was being watched. That someone would bust in any moment and haul him away.

He returned to the album. Sitting on his bed, he replaced the photo and looked quickly through the album for any more hidden messages. Finding none, he studied his room, looking for some place to hide the album and the note. Quillon remembered Morgan waiting around for him to open it. *Was he told to find out what was in the envelope?* he thought. Finally, he decided to just leave it in plain sight on the table.

He walked around the room a few times, worrying about what to do about Jackson's original note. *Maybe I should tear that up and flush it as well,* he thought. *That won't work. Morgan already knows about it.*

Quillon read the note several more times, trying to decide if there was anything in it that suggested at the existence of the hidden message. He could feel his anxiety rising. He had taken his pills this morning but took another pill because he could feel the tightness in his chest.

Finally, he could not stand it anymore. "I need some fresh air," he said loudly, partly to hear himself think, but mostly to explain his actions, just in case someone was listening.

Quillon waved to the two officers inside the security office while he waited for the elevator. He never really got to know the second shift since he had gotten back from his meetings late and when straight to bed. The two officers nodded and continued their conversation. Quillon guessed the other must be in the cafeteria. He gladly stepped into the elevator and tapped his card several times on the panel, but got no response.

Quillon stepped partly out of the elevator and shouted. "What's up with the elevator? None of the lights work."

"There's nothing wrong with the elevator," said an officer in the security office.

"Then there must be something wrong with my card," said Quillon, as he tried to elevator panel again. Frustrated, Quillon slammed his palm on the elevator's wall just above the control panel.

"Hey, knock that off," came a stern warning.

"Sorry," said Quillon, stepping out of the elevator and holding his card up. "I think this card is messed up."

"Have you used it today" asked the shift supervisor who had come out of the cafeteria because of the noise.

"Yes," said Quillon. "But it is not working now. None of the buttons are working," he said, pointing toward the elevator.

"The card is working. Sounds like your access had changed," said the supervisor as he headed back into the cafeteria.

"That can't be," shouted Quillon, toward the supervisor. "I had it changed yesterday."

"Well, then it must have been changed again today," said one officer in the office.

"Then change it back," shouted Quillon.

"I think you should return to your room and calm down before you get in trouble," said the supervisor, returning to the hallway, this time with his hand on his taser.

One of the other two officers stepped out of their office, hand also on his taser.

"Sorry," said Quillon as he realized they were not really listening to him. "I just wanted the access changed," he said toward the supervisor while retreating toward his room. "Can you check to see if there was a mistake?"

"There is no mistake," said the supervisor, who had reached the elevator and was joined by an officer.

Quillon saw the officer in the room pick up the phone. He pointed toward the man and said, "Then can I speak to someone else about it? Can you get Stephanus on the phone?"

"The Director is busy with the regent meeting. We will let him know about your concerns," said the supervisor, hand still on his taser. "In the meantime, I'm instructing you to return to your room. If I feel you can behave yourself, we will let you visit the recreation room."

Quillon had heard that kind of talk at one of the hospitals he had spent time in. He knew where this was heading, so decided the only thing he could do was do what they said.

Once inside his room, he heard a clunk he had not heard before. Returning to the door, he found his card did not open it. He stepped back several feet, just staring at the door. Quillon felt an anger building inside until he just let it out with a scream. He returned to his bed and shouted, hoping someone was listing, "Has everyone gone mad? You can't do this to me!"

Quillon felt his chest ache. He put his hand on it and said, "No, not now. I don't want another dream."

He closed his eyes and tried to relax. He felt a slight burning and when he opened his eyes, Henrietta was standing several feet from him. She was staring at him, like always, but for the first time, there was a smile on her face. It reminded him of the smile he had seen on her in the vision. Quillon held up his hand and begged, "Please, Henrietta, I'm sorry." She did not move, but continued to smile at him. He wasn't sure why, but he could feel the pain in his chest lessen until it was gone. Quillon took a deep breath and felt a sense of ease, both his pain and his anger slowly leaving him. He looked back at Henrietta and said, "Thank you," and with that, she vanished.

Chapter 21
Just Enough Rope

Georges didn't mind speaking in front of large groups. He often sponsored a literary conference each year. He loved the chance to talk about any new interpretation of a line of ancient text or hear about the newest methods of seeing into old and fragile scrolls. There was even the great discussion last year on a new computerized method of analyzing similarities in authorship between different unnamed documents. This kind of meeting, however, was not one of those he enjoyed. Any meeting of the foundation regents was sure to be full of arguments and power struggles. He knew a few of the people present were looking for any opportunity to have him removed. He would have to be very careful in his explanation of why he had limited their access to his most recent discoveries.

The meeting was setup in the larger of the Foundation's two video conference areas. This room was much like a lecture room. There were three rows of long curved desks, each higher than the other. Set into the desks were video monitors. The room was equipped with three large video screens, side by side. To the right was a little media control center and a couple of smaller chairs.

After some polite conversation, Georges took his place behind a thin modern podium that rose from the floor when needed. It was positioned at the far right side of the room, slightly in front of the media center. It gave Georges a view of the auditorium seats and the screens.

Georges tapped on the microphone, and the seven visiting regents took their places in the front row, and Stephanus found a chair in one of the remaining rows.

The large screen to the left flickered, and then filled with the faces of the remaining six regents. Georges looked at the collection of faces and, after a quick head count, asked, "Are we ready?" A quick series of nods from the video screen followed.

Georges looked around, then said, "Gentleman." He paused for a few seconds, clicked his controller, and the center screen filled with an image of the library with the swirling dark portal fixed in the center of the screen. "I give to you a bit of Stolen Madness."

All the Regents had read reports on the portal, but seeing it now, larger than life, brought the reaction that Georges expected. He paused to once again admire the beauty of the portal, before flicking the controller to zoom in until the portal filled the screen.

"There, in the darkness, you'll see evidence of movement." Georges watched the faces on the monitor as they studied the screen. When he saw he had their attention again, he said, "You should have a copy of my latest report on the progress in controlling this event. I'm sure you will notice the comments on staff changes. As part of our effort to understand some of the unusual elements of this event, specifically the psychic link between Quillon and the appearance of an entity he described as his sister, we brought in an expert in the fields of Parapsychology and Paranormal studies. After extensive evaluation, she has concluded that none of these secondary events were related to her field of study. With that hurtle cleared, Regent Elliott will continue with our evaluation of the magical influences. I'm sure you're eager to learn what he has planned, so I'm turning the podium over to him."

Georges had notified Elliott of his renewed status in the project only a few moments prior to the start of the meeting. Actually, he had his assistant contact Elliott's assistant, hoping the short notice would limit the time for Elliott to organize a critical assault on the project and his position. Still, he was surprised and a little worried to see Elliot already wheeling toward the podium before Georges could finish his introduction.

Elliot calmly adjusted the height of the podium, placed a folder of notes on it, and took his time adjusting the microphone. "Thank you, Grand Master Georges, fellow Regents." He allowed the heads on the screen to nod their greetings. Elliot signaled to the media control area and the screen to the right of the center screen lit up with a set of PowerPoint notes. It contained the name for the meeting, his name, and a simple agenda which had three items: Cause, Current Status, Options for Closure.

With a click of the controller, the next screen appeared with a header of **Cause** and a brief statement that read, "*An unauthorized summoning was conducted when sensitive, highly restricted items were made available for general access.*"

Georges shifted slightly in his chair. He had hoped the meeting wouldn't degrade into name calling, but he was prepared if that happened. He was relieved when he heard Elliot say, "For now, I would like to leave discussion of that for another time. I think it would be best to review our current situation and our options going forward."

Elliot clicked the control again and the words **Current Status** followed by a bullet point and the words **Summoning Site Containment** were displayed. Elliot adjusted the microphone again and said, "It may not look like it, but separate from the efforts of the Grand Master, my department, at significant risk, has made substantial progress. We have used our considerable knowledge to help ensure the safety of all members of the Foundation. All the surfaces surrounding the portal now have wards on them. Cameras, microphones, and other physical monitoring devices have been protected from magical attack. We have also, without the help or suggestion of the current team leadership, established teams that are constantly monitoring the energy and activity within the library and the building itself. Because of these actions, I can report that the summoning site is stable."

He clicked the controller again. A green check mark appeared next to the first bullet point, and another one appeared below it that said, '*Summoning Situation Evaluation.*'

"My department has spent hours reviewing data related to summoning and has determined that this one is unique. All summoning requires a circle, which acts as a focus and container for the summoned entity. The only suggestion of a portal linked to summoning, instead of a circle, is in the Surowiecki papers, much of which is untranslated."

"Still, it is the unanimous decision of my department that the portal works much in the same way as a summoning circle. We also feel the current situation has characteristics similar to any failed or improperly conducted summoning. This means that we should focus on the summoning spell for the entity. We feel the portal is just the visualization of that spell. Allowing the spell to properly complete would give us the intended access and, I'm sure, control of the creature. The other route would be to destroy the spell, which should cause both the portal and entity to vanish."

There was a ding, and a green light appeared next to Yuri's chair. "You have a question already, Regent Lebedev?"

"You realize that the creature you are talking about is the one referred to as the Stolen Madness," said Yuri. "I am concerned that you are so casually talking about controlling this thing."

"As I have stated before, and anyone that has training in these areas knows, what is inside a summoning circle cannot leave that circle unless it is broken and that is not something either myself or my team is going to let happen," said Elliott. "As you can see from my outline, the real question is what do we do with it once we have control of it?"

There was another soft ding, and a green dot appeared beside a face on the screen. "Regent Donavon, you also have a question?" asked Elliot.

Regent Donavon spoke with a heavy English accent and said, "Regent Elliot, do you have any explanations for the tattoo and how they're connected to the summoning?"

Elliott repositioned himself and said, "Markings and symbols are often used in ceremonies to either strengthen a spell or protect the caster. It is unusual for them to be created instead of drawn. This is obviously a very sophisticated and powerful spell. It is my belief it is intended to protect the summoner. Since the summoning has not completed, it is still working, probably to protect Quillon from the danger of the blood loss he is experiencing. Once again, amazing example of magic at work."

"Interesting suggestion," said Georges. He was glad to hear that Elliot had not discovered what he believed was the true nature of the tattoos.

Elliott paused, glanced at Georges, as if he was waiting for some other remark to follow, then said, "Now, if we can return to the discussion on how to move forward."

When there were no further interruptions, Elliot clicked again and the words '**Options for Closure**,' appeared in a font larger than the last. "That brings us to today's discussion. What to do with the results of this unauthorized summoning? Both my department and some members of this council feel there are only three choices available to us." He clicked, and the words, '*Close the Portal*', '*Keep it Open*', and '*Make it Someone Else's Problem*' appeared.

Before Elliot could cover the points on the screen, there was another ding. Elliot's struggles with the interruption were showing as he said, "You have another question, Regent Donavon?"

"Regent Elliott, the reports I've read said our attempts to close the portal failed. It appears from the screen that you have determined some alternative way of closing it?"

"That's correct Regent Donavon. Earlier attempts failed. We were not made fully aware that fragments of the dagger were feeding off a blood source and keeping the portal open." Elliot pointed toward Professor Georges and said, "The Grand Master has expressed his agreement with my assessment that the portal will close once the source of blood is removed."

"And is there anyway of removing this blood source without a loss of life?" asked Donavon.

"I would refer that question to the Grand Master since I have not been privy to all the projects information. Especially anything related to the medical conditions of Quillon," said Elliot.

Georges remained seated and said, "The answer to your question is no. Quillon's records show that when he was first hospitalized, the fragments were distinct enough to remove, but his health prevented any attempts to remove them. By the time Quillon was transferred here, the fragments were merged with surrounding bone and any chance of removal was impossible."

"And what is his long-term prognosis?" asked Donavon.

"The results of the fragments feeding on him have made him anemic. There are also the effects of the growing tattoo, which also impact his blood flow. The doctors refuse to give an end date since they are not sure how best to treat him, or even if that treatment would prolong that date. They said that if the conditions do not change, even with treatment, Quillon could suffer critical organ failure."

There was the sound of another bell ringing and a green light displayed on the desk in front of Regent Wellington. Donavon said, "I yield the floor."

"When Quillon dies, will we be able to recover the fragments from his body and use them in a way to better manage the portal?" asked Wellington.

Elliot said, "I've created magical items before. Many are extremely sophisticated. Given time and access to the proper resource, I'm sure I can repair or recreate the dagger. If not, it is my hope the Surowiecki papers contain information on how to recreate it."

"Well, if that is possible, let's get on with it. Close the gate, make a dagger, problem solved," said Ashwin. "Then we can talk about selling this thing to someone else."

"I agree," said Regent Wellington. "I recommend we allow the test subject to expire, then have Regent Elliot and his people create a replacement dagger."

"I can speak to that," said Georges, without pausing for permission.

"Go ahead, Grand Master," said Elliot. "Is there some additional hidden information that your studies can provide?"

"I have been busy analyzing the Surowiecki papers using some exciting new technology. I was able to learn more about the creation of the dagger. However, I need to point out there is still some confusion about the purpose of the dagger. Doctor Taylor presented an interesting idea that the portal is some kind of containment for the creature and not a summoning circle.

"I think we can agree that Doctor Taylor, while an expert in her own field, is not the person we should take advice on magic from," said Elliott. There was a slight chuckle from his supporters in the front row. "I recognize your abilities in document research, but unfortunately, I need to point out your limited knowledge in summoning magic. There are no records of something like a containment portal and it would not even make sense. That is what the summoning circle is for."

Georges let out a little sigh for effect. He finally had Elliott where he wanted him. "Her explanation sounded reasonable at the time."

"I told you before," said Elliot loudly, "This is a summoning, not a sideshow act. It was created through magic and needs to be addressed by those that truly understand magic. Not a bunch of hippies."

"Gentlemen please," came the voice of Regent Wickmayer. "If we can return to some level of order and civility. Grand Master, I believe you were going to provide information on creating the summoning dagger."

"You're right, Regent Wickmayer. I'm sorry Elliot," said Georges. He rubbed his beard, doing his best to hide a smile now that he had gotten Elliott to publicly deny Taylor's theory. Now he just needed to weaken Elliot's position. Once he had his smile under control, he said, "I feel confident that, in time, once we've translated more of the papers, Regent Elliot could create a replacement dagger. However, there's one thing that he doesn't appear to be aware of."

"What's that?" asked Elliot.

"As you know, the Foundation designated the dagger and Necro Box as forbidden," said Georges, waiting for the question he knew would follow.

"Why would it being designated forbidden have anything to do with me creating a replacement dagger?" asked Elliot.

"My research into the reason for the classification revealed that the dagger was created through the combined efforts of three high-ranking mages, basically the equivalent of our Regents. The casting took several days. Shortly after, all three died. The notes said their bodies were covered with horrible wounds, like welts, and they were drained of blood."

The room was quiet for several minutes until a bell sounded. The quietness made the ring sound louder.

"Regent Wickmayer, please, your thoughts," said Elliot.

"Thank you," Wickmayer spoke slowly and softly. "The death of Quillon and the closing of the portal are, it appears, destined to happen. It also appears that the idea of creating a replacement dagger is out of the question. I think we can all agree that we are fortunate the summoning happened the way it did. It allowed us to evaluate the results without all the death that must have occurred the first time it was summoned. I would say that this forbidden magic is a bust. Worthless. Unless anyone can suggest a reason that would make repeating the summons in the future meaningful?"

A few seconds later Stephanus raised his hand and after a surprised Elliott acknowledged him, he said, "The idea of communicating mentally with the creature suggests several exciting opportunities, but does not ensure control over its movements. As long as it is stationary, it's useless as a weapon."

"Interesting point, and one that begs the question of why we would want to control it in the first place? Thank you for your insight, Director," said Wickmayer.

After a short pause, when no other comments were forwarded, Wickmayer said, "I can't think of anything that warrants the price of continuing the study once the portal closes. Therefore, I make a motion that Regent Elliot continue with his efforts to close the portal, however I believe the Grand Master should still manage the project overall. I also make a motion that when it shuts down, either on its own or with our help, we destroy everything associated with it, including the Surowiecki papers, the Necro Box, the dagger, and any fragments recovered from Quillon's body. They labeled this Forbidden Magic for a valid reason, and it's time we acknowledged that."

There was a call to second the motion, and a vote was called. Georges sat watching the results of the meeting unfold in the way he had expected. Soon, green lights were lit beside each of the faces on the monitor and the seats next to him. When he heard Elliot say "Pass" and call for an end to the meeting, he felt a bit relieved that his leadership held. He was more excited that he had kept his secrets about the true nature of the Necro Box while still being able to say he tried to tell them.

Georges had already prepared material prior to the meeting that should now be on its way to Elliot's office. It would take him days to root through it. Georges chuckled, thinking of poor Elliott stumbling around trying to catch up, and too proud to ask for help. Georges would have the time he needed to continue working on the only thing that really mattered. The magic that controlled the Necro Box.

Watching Elliot chatting with his cronies, Georges did his best to hide a smile. He would let Elliot play with his monster, but he needed to get busy. That meant he would need to convince Quillon to take more risky actions before Elliot could figure out a way to take control of him. "Time to spill the beans," Georges said in a whisper as he headed back toward his office.

Chapter 22
Spilled Beans

Quillon studied his image in the mirror. He felt tired, almost as tired as the face in the mirror looked. Quillon squeezed his cheeks, pulling at the dark bags under his eyes. He thought about putting a comb through his hair to remove the sleep from it, but right now, that felt like too much work.

He wondered how long he had been sleeping. Without a window, it was hard for him to judge the time of day. Henrietta's visit had been shortly after breakfast. He had paced around the room about fifty times, checking the door each time he passed. Finally, he just gave up, laid down and went to sleep.

Now that he was up, Quillon wondered what he should do next. *There must be someway to use that intercom to call out,* he thought That got him thinking about the message light. It was off. His stomach said it should be on by now. *I wonder if they're going to let me know when it was time to eat,* he thought. *They can't starve me.*

He continued to stare at the door until his stomach grumbled again. *That's it,* he thought. He grabbed his card and headed for the door. *If it doesn't open this time, I'm going to bang on it until someone comes.* To his surprise, the door opened.

Quillon stepped out into the hallway and saw no one. He stepped back in and tried the door a few more times, just to be sure. Each time it worked, he felt the anger and tension lessen. Watching the door open and close reminded him of the elevator. *I need some fresh air,* he thought. *Then I need to talk to someone about this mess.* Looking down, he remembered he hadn't changed his clothes since they had locked him in. *Better get cleaned up first.*

He quickly showered, changed, and was just getting ready to leave when the call button on the door sounded. He paused for a second, deciding if he should ignore it, but finally gave in. "Hello?"

"Quillon, is that you?" said the voice, which he recognized as Georges.

"Yes, it's me." he replied. Once he let go of the button, he mumbled sarcastically, "Who else would be locked in here?"

"I'm sorry about the mix-up with the access," said Georges.

Quillon froze. He wondered if Georges had heard his last comment.

"When we turned off the access to Doctor Taylor's office, you must have been caught up in that," continued Georges. "I have restored your access to the first floor."

"That's nice," said Quillon. "I hope someone had a word with your security. They threatened me and locked me in my room."

"That's unfortunate," said Georges. "I will look into it."

Unfortunate, thought Quillon. *Try illegal.*

The intercom was silent, and Quillon wondered if Georges was finished. "Are you still there?" he asked.

"Yes," said Georges. "I was just on the other line, leaving a message for my assistant to look into your complaint."

"Thank you, Professor," said Quillon. "If there's nothing else, I would like to get a little fresh air, now that I can."

"There is another matter I need to discuss with you," said Georges. "I've given you access to reach my office."

"Does it need to be right now?" Quillon asked.

"I'm afraid this discussion has waited too long," said Georges. "Time is of the essence. We can talk about Mr. Jackson's letter when you get here."

Quillon stiffened at the mention of his letter. He hurried to the album, reached for it, but stopped. Quillon wasn't sure, but it looked like the album had been moved. He tried to remember how he had left it. *This place is getting to me,* he thought, then quickly found Jackson's letter where he had left it. Still holding the album, he looked back at the intercom.

"This is a serious matter, Quillon," said Georges. "It would be best for both of us if you came now."

The light on the intercom turned off. Quillon stared at it for a few seconds then said, "Professor, how do I get to your office?"

There was no answer.

Quillon thought about what Georges had said. If he hadn't mentioned the letter, Quillon would have put off the meeting. He hadn't even eaten yet. But the mention of the letter irritated him. *I bet Morgan said something,"* he thought as he headed for the elevator.

He hesitated, tapping the panel, mostly because it would remind him that Jackson and his sister were gone. When he tapped it, the buttons for his floor, the first floor and 3A lit up.

3A, what the heck is that? He wondered as he pressed it. It didn't take long to find out. It startled him when the back of the elevator opened to reveal a small lobby.

A man in his late twenties, wearing a nice dark blue suit with a salmon colored tie, rose from his desk, pointed to a collection of minimalist styled chairs and said, "My name is Hayward, the Grand Master's assistant. Have a seat, Mr. Thomas. I'll let him know you're here."

The little lobby was impressive. There was lots of glass with dark wood accents. One of the glass walls had a stunning view of the forest. Across from it, was another glass wall, with the room entrance. The walkway just outside of the lobby had a glass wall of its own that gave just a hint of a splendid view of the lobby below. The wood-paneled wall behind Hayward's desk was decorated with several framed magazines covers and awards. In the center was a crest which Quillon guessed belonged to the Foundation. He didn't recognize the language, but he recognized a golden pyramid in the center.

The wall behind him was decorated with thirteen portraits next to the elevator door. The men were all dressed in ceremonial outfits. It was obvious some portraits were completed some time ago. Quillon picked out the portrait of Georges, even though it showed him at least twenty years younger. As Quillon scanned the portraits, another looked vaguely familiar. It was a powerful looking man in his early thirties, with shoulder length dark hair and a goatee. The name on the plaque was Dr. Jordan Elliott. Quillon didn't recognize the name, but there was something familiar about the man; maybe the eyes.

Quillon was studying the other portraits when he heard Georges come out of his office.

"Good," he said. "You're ready to go."

Quillon knew the professor had the box and dagger without needing to turn around. He felt it. When he turned, Georges was just a few feet from him and reaching for the elevator call button, the box was tucked under his left arm.

"Our Board of Regents," said Georges, nodding towards the paintings. "I guess I should update my portrait, but I kind of like that one. They needed me to sit for three days. I guess nowadays they just take a picture and make it look like a painting. Sometimes, when things look too real, they lose something."

The elevator opened and before Quillon could say anything, Georges stepped in and said, "Let's go. We have little time. As Quillon followed, Georges said, tell me what Mr. Jackson said in his letter."

"How did you know about the letter?" asked Quillon as the elevator door closed behind him.

"It's my job to know what happens here. It's something I work hard at."

"Basically, they left because they couldn't help me. It was not their kind of thing," said Quillon.

The elevator stopped, and Quillon saw they were on the first floor. "Are we going outside for a walk?" he asked hopefully.

"This way," said Georges, as he headed toward the door Quillon knew led to the main lobby and the library beyond it. "Tell me about the other letter."

Quillon felt a chill at George's comment. *They must be watching me,* he thought. He followed quietly along behind, hoping Georges would not ask again.

"I'm a document researcher, and a good one," said Georges, standing at the door that opened into the lobby. "I specialize in spotting cryptic references. Mr. Jackson's were not that subtle. He warned you about being watched and told you were to find more information. Correct?"

Quillon used to think he was good at lying to authorities, but his counselors had proved to him otherwise. He knew Georges would see through any attempt to get around the truth. He also believed that Georges would not open that door until he confessed. Quillon took a deep breath, let it out slowly, then said, "It said they quit because it was too dangerous. The dreams are real, and I should trust my sister."

"Good. That saves me the trouble of telling you the same thing," said Georges, as he stood, hand still on the handle of the lobby door.

Quillon just stared at Georges, not sure what he had heard.

Jackson's comments about his dreams, both in the lab and in the letter, he had finally put down as wishful thinking from a ghost hunter. Hearing the Grand Master of a secret magical society saying much the same thing got his head spinning.

"Did you recognize anyone else in the regent paintings?" asked Georges, still standing with his hand on the door handle.

Quillon was getting uncomfortable and wished Georges would open the door so they could step into the large open lobby he knew was on the other side. Hoping that an answer would get them moving again, he said, "A regent named Elliott looked familiar, but truthfully, I wasn't sure I recognized you until I checked the nameplate."

"Good," said Georges, as he opened the door and stepped through. He paused on the other side and, before moving enough to allow Quillon to enter, said, "That painting of Regent Elliott was from a different time in his life. We used to be almost friends once. Unfortunately, you will probably meet him again in the next few days. He is not a man to anger. Remember that."

"I have never met him before," said Quillon as he made his way into the lobby. Once inside, he found the lobby to be very different from the one he visited on the night of the party.

In daylight, with the absences of partygoers and party décor, the space looked gigantic. It reminded him more of the lobby of an expensive hotel than a business, complete with scattered seating areas and a coffee bar. The major difference from the night of the party was the construction. There was a wooden wall that ran the length of the far side with 'Pardon our Dust' painted on it.

At the place where he remembered the hallway to the library was a door in the wall, two security officers, and a little podium with a laptop.

"Actually, you've met Regent Elliott before," said Georges. "He was the man in the wheelchair you saw in the dream where you watched Hugo die."

Quillon shook his head slightly and wanted to deny Georges' accusation, but the eyes in the painting came back to him. Mentally, he attempted several arguments against what was quickly becoming a horrible reality. "That means I really was there," he finally said, almost in a whisper.

"I thought you took Mr. Jackson's letter seriously," said Georges, as he walked off in the direction of the construction wall. He paused after a few feet and said, "This way. Come on, we need to hurry."

Quillon followed while he thought about the dreams. A sickening thought came to him, and he blurted out, "That means I killed them!" He stopped as soon as he said it, looking around.

"No, that thing did. You were just along for the ride," said Georges.

Quillon stopped several times during the short distance it took to join Georges at the security post.

"Show him your card," said Georges.

"Where are we going?" Quillon asked as he handed the officer his card.

Georges smiled and calmly said, "It's time to face your dreams."

Chapter 23
You're Kidding Right?

Once through the gate for the construction wall, Quillon saw the space beyond had a ceiling that was not visible from the floor level. He guessed it was to keep people from the upper floors from seeing what lie ahead of him.

The old library hallway was gone, and Quillon stood before what he could only describe as an airlock. It looked like it was made of clear plastic and came complete with armed guards on both sides.

Quillon paused, his mind and feet both not sure where he was supposed to be going. "What's that?" he asked.

"Protection," said Georges. He tapped his card against a panel built into the entrance and the door on this side slid open. Georges step to the side, held out the box towards Quillon, and said "Take this."

Quillon reached out for the box and then stopped. "Why, what do I need that for?" he said, glancing nervously between the box, the hallway, and the guards.

"We need you to close the portal." said Georges as he pushed the box into Quillon's hands, then pointing toward the hallway he said, "Take this. Go down to the library and do what your sister showed you."

"I'm not going in there. If my dreams are real, like you and Jackson said, that thing will kill me," said Quillon as he attempted to hand the box back to Georges.

"Maybe," said Georges, "But I can guarantee you will die if you don't go in."

Quillon was not expecting that. He stood up straight, forgetting he was still holding the box, and asked, "Why am I going to die if I stay out here?"

"I guess I'm going to have to explain things to you after all," said Georges, taking the box. "Think about the dream your sister gave you. The dagger in here, and the bits in your chest use blood, your blood, to summon that portal," said Georges, pointing in the library's direction. "Every time it takes blood from you, it grows and if it grows enough, that thing is going to escape."

Quillon nodded, hearing most of this for the first time. Placing his hand on his chest he said, "You're saying if I stay out here, it's going to bleed me to death?"

"No, I'm saying the regents of this foundation voted to kill you, hoping that would shut off the supply of blood to the dagger and close the portal."

"Kill me," said Quillon, looking around at the armed guards but found no expression of sympathy. "You can't do that. It's illegal. Besides, people know I'm here."

"Secret, powerful society, remember," said Georges, shaking his head slightly. "We have done so in the past and will do so again if necessary. As for your friends, we never leave loose ends."

Quillon felt the panic grow inside. He looked around for some place to run and saw there was no way out. "There must be another way. Talk to them."

"That's why we are here. While I agree killing you might be the easiest solution, I wanted to give you a chance to close the portal on your own," said Georges.

Quillon looked down the hallway, then back to Georges, and asked, "How am I supposed to do that?"

"I believe the answer is in the vision your sister showed you. Use the dagger to command the portal to close."

"It didn't work for Hugo," said Quillon. "What makes you think this is going to work for me?"

"Hugo didn't have all the pieces of the dagger and he did not have the box," said Georges. "We also did not have the benefit of your last vision where the true nature of the box was revealed. Use what she showed you. When the portal is closed, put the dagger back in the box and make sure it stays shut."

"You really think I can figure out how to close this thing?" asked Quillon.

"You opened it," said Georges, who paused, then reached in his pocket and pulled out several loops. Offering them to Quillon, he said, "If not, use these."

"Rubber bands! You're kidding, right?"

"We can worry about how to keep it closed later. For now, we go with whatever is easiest for you to use."

Quillon looked around at the armed guards, then back at the rubber bands in Georges' outstretched hand. He could feel his hand shaking as he reached for them. "Whose going with me?"

"It needs to be only you," said Georges. "We don't want to give that creature any reason to ignore you."

Quillon hesitated a bit when Georges offered the box. He tucked it under his arm, making sure he held the lid closed. Looking down the hallway, he asked, "How long do I need to stay in there?"

"It was your dream. You should know better than anyone how long it will take," said Georges.

"So let me get this straight. I walk in, open the box, shout begone three times, and when the portal vanishes, I close the box and put the rubber bands around it." When Georges nodded his approval, Quillon asked, "Do I need to say anything special or speak in Latin?"

"Do you know Latin?" asked Georges, with a look of curiosity on his face.

"No, it's just in all the movies they use Latin to chase off the demons."

Georges let out a short laugh that ended in a soft chuckle. "That just shows what they know," said Georges with a smile. "Keep it simple. It is the intent of the command that matters. Now it's time to get started."

The guards opened the second door at Georges' signal, and, with the aid of a slight push, Quillon walked through it. He could see a single chair in the middle of the hallway about 20 feet in front of him.

He held the box tight, almost like he was carrying a football, and advanced slowly towards the chair. It was a simple metal chair, and it was bathed in light. As Quillon got closer, he realized the light was coming from inside the library through what looked like a thick glass barrier. He was glad to see that it looked much stronger than the one he had knocked down before.

Quillon stopped, just thinking of the last time he had been here. He got a chill when he saw the dried bloodstains on the floor and carpet. As he looked at each, the memory of the owner and their death returned to him.

Looking back toward the lobby, Quillon was not surprised to see that door closed. "No way out now," he muttered as he inched toward the chair.

Standing in front of the opening to the library, there was no way of pretending the portal beyond the inches of clear protection was only a dream. It was larger than he imagined. In his dreams, he had been on the other side of it, but it always appears smaller. At least that's the impression he got. There it was, the opening at least six feet wide and the whole thing floating at least three feet off the floor. The top of it almost touched the ceiling.

When Quillon had first seen the barrier separating the hallway from the library, he worried the creature could not hear him command it to leave. As he stood inches away, that worry was replaced with a fear that the barrier was not thick enough.

The sounds from the portal were much stronger on this side of his dreams. He listened to the hissing sound of the dark clouds as they appeared to come from behind the edge of the portal, out of nowhere, and spill into the portal opening. The ground below the portal was stained with a dark slime from where the clouds touched.

The barrier failed to hold back the smell of rancid air that flowed freely from the world beyond the opening. The smell had been hard to handle in his dreams, but here it was even worse. He gagged several times, stepping back into the chair behind him. No matter how hard he struggled, he could not hold back. He placed the box on the chair and stepped behind it, and vomited several times.

He breathed slowly, still fighting back the urge to vomit again. When he thought he had it under control, he turned back to the library and froze, unable to move.

The barrier in front of him was covered with what looked like tentacles of varying sizes. Some had flat tips that contained small mouths that gnawed at the barrier. All of them moved and squirmed as if each had a mind of its own. He had not even heard them approaching. They did not appear to be trying to break through, more like they were testing, investigating. Seeing them from the other side of his dreams, he never feared them. Here, seeing them this close, he had to struggle to breathe.

Slowly, he reached for the box on the chair. The tentacles seem to follow his movement slightly. When he picked up the box, some of them retreated, enough for him to see how the bundle of them was squeezed through the opening of the portal. The ones not at the entrance spread throughout the library, each searching. Some were pressed against the walls, others the ceiling, the rest spread around and over the bookshelf and cabinets.

Quillon held the box up in front of him and placed his hand on the lid. When he did so, more of the tentacles retreated and two large ones slammed against the barrier, causing Quillon to drop the box.

He could feel the change in the room, as if all the tentacles turned their attention to him. Quillon glanced down and saw the dagger had tumbled out of the box. He stared at it and felt a desire to hold it. A desire so strong it replaced the fear he had of the tentacles just feet from him. As he reached for it, he could almost feel the tentacles beyond the barrier doing the same.

As he wrapped his hand around the handle, he felt the pain start. A sharp pain that traveled up his arm to the wound on his chest. He felt the heat and itching of the tattoo start as well. Somehow, he found the chair and as he sat, he could see the portal pulse with each throb of his wound. He wanted to drop the dagger but could not. The next pain was stronger. He took a deep breath and closed his eyes.

When he opened them again, Quillon saw himself sitting in a chair, slumped down, holding an open box on his lap. His other arm was held above his head, the dagger clenched in his fist.

Anger filled Quillon's mind; an uncontrollable anger. He had felt this anger in the past, but now it was greater than before and seemed to grow with each pulse.

He felt a strong desire to reach out for the dagger. He could feel the pulses of his heart and saw the portal struggling to widen.

Quillon watched as two large tentacles raised before him, like snakes ready to attack, their tips pointing at the barrier. He felt the urge to strike at the barrier. To crush the hated thing on the other side. Quillon's mind went back to the last time he was in this room and he knew what waited for his body sitting on the other side.

At first Quillon felt fear and helplessness. Those feelings were soon replaced by anger. Quillon hated not being in control. He hated the creature. As his hate grew, he felt something strange. It was fear, but it was not his. Quillon realized the creature was responding to his hate.

He felt a weakness in the urge to pound on the barrier. Quillon directed all his hate at those wavering arms and felt a great relief when they fell limp to the ground.

Quillon's relief was short-lived as he heard a roar and knew another mind was responsible for that. The anger returned, but instead of being directed at the barrier and what was beyond, it was directed toward him and it scared him. In those few seconds, he felt his control over the tentacles slipping.

Please, someone help me, Quillon thought over and over, as if it would protect him from that anger. It was then that he felt the burning. His head hurt and he felt sleepy. His eyes would close and each time he opened them, the view was different. He found himself drifting between the dream where he was looking at himself and the view from the chair.

The burning on his chest was growing stronger and soon became more painful than the sharp, pulsing pain. As the burning increased, his head cleared. He opened his eyes and saw himself sitting in the chair with the box on his lap and the dagger still being held about his head. *It's a dream,* he thought. *I just need to wake up.* He closed his eyes again and when they opened, he was still looking at himself in the chair, but beside him was Henrietta.

The deep anger that boiled just below his control changed. It was suddenly mixed with a new feeling, one of fear. He realized that the source of the fear was Henrietta. Fear mix with anger soon became panic, and he felt himself losing control of the tentacles. Several appeared to be suspended in air, like snakes, ready to strike.

Quillon watched as Henrietta reached up and placed her hand on his arm that was still raised, clutching the dagger. She slowly moved his arm down towards his lap and the waiting box. Soon Quillon's own fear mixed with that of the creature's, causing the tentacles to pull back.

The combination of the burning which now was becoming unbearable, and the feeling of fear and panic made Quillon wish he was someplace else, anywhere but here. His room, deep in the basement, was the only place he could think of. The thought surprised him since he had never really thought of it as his, but the idea of a locking door and guards in the hallway made it feel a lot safer than here.

He closed his mind and thought about his room, the simple bedroom, the closet, bathroom, and that door, the locking one, without a doorknob. Quillon could almost see it, close enough to touch. He reached out and felt a chill run through him when he saw tentacles tapping on the door.

Quillon quickly looked around as best he could. To his right, in the bathroom, he could just make out the mirror. There, inside, was the reflection of the portal. It was smaller than before and there were fewer arms extending through it.

The pulse in his chest started again, and Quillon knew the portal was struggling to widen. His worries about the portal were soon overshadowed by the burning and itching. The pain it caused made him want to scream. When he thought he would pass out, he closed his eyes.

When he opened them again, he was sitting in the chair in front of the library, now empty. Quillon looked down at his lap and saw the box wrapped in rubber bands. He also saw his right arm, the one with the hand that held the dagger, was covered with the tattoo. It had spread to his wrist. He watched as the color faded to a faint red.

Noise in the hallway caught his attention. When he looked, he saw Georges and four armed guards heading his way. He looked back into the library, trying to remember all that had happened.

"I have some help on the way," said Georges, as he quickly retrieved the box from Quillon's lap, then quickly stepped back to allow the guards to inspect the interior of the library.

"It's not here anymore," Quillon mumbled.

"That's great. Looks like it worked," said Georges.

"I'm so tired," said Quillon.

"We will get you to the clinic," said Georges. "They will check you out. After that, you can spend all day in your room resting."

"No!" said Quillon, thinking about what now waited in his room. "It's not in the library anymore! You said I could go if it went away." The last few words barely left his lips before the fatigue overcame him.

Chapter 24
Valuable Yes, Safe No

Quillon remembered little of what happened after he moved the portal to his room. He knew he was back in the clinic and was glad he didn't wake up in his room. He wondered if anyone had found that thing waiting there.

His head hurt, and he was having trouble with his vision. He reached to rub his eyes and quickly discovered the restraints.

"What's going on?" he asked of the nurse who was sitting nearby. "What's happening to me?"

"Good, you're awake," said the nurse. "I'll let them know."

"Let me up," said Quillon, trying to move.

"Don't do that," said the nurse. "You might pull something out."

That's when he discovered that besides restraints, he had gained an IV and a catheter.

Quillon stopped struggling and said, "Why are you doing this? I did what I was told."

The nurse ignored him as she returned to her little office. Quillon could see her making a phone call.

"If you don't let me go, you're going to be sorry," shouted Quillon. The nurse just looked his way briefly as she continued her call.

It was then that he noticed a dark suited security officer standing at the door. "Hey you! Go get the Professor for me." The man glanced his way, then looked away. "Help, help me, someone," shouted Quillon. He smiled when he saw the nurse walking his way. "Good, hurry or when I get out of this, you're going to be sorry."

Quillon watched as the nurse injected something into the IV. He felt a warmth running through his arm and his mouth got dry. He wanted to speak, but before he could, the world darkened.

QUILLON blinked at the light. It took him a few seconds to realize he had been sleeping again. No, not sleeping, drugged. He took a deep breath and looked around. He found he was lying on a gurney, but was still restrained. The location was different, and there was no one in the room. He looked around as best he could, trying to figure out where he was. It was not the clinic or any of the other rooms he had visited. The space was quite roomy and looked like some kind of control room. From where he lay, he could make out a console with several small screens, like what he would expect in a TV studio. There were also a couple of large flat screens mounted on the walls and a large window through which he could just make out the roof of another room. He could not see all of it, but what he could see was covered with several strange symbols.

Quillon shouted a few times but got no answer. While he was testing his restraints, there was the sound of a door opening behind him and he shouted, "Who's there? What's going on?"

"We have you restrained, both as a precaution, and for everyone's protection," came a man's voice from behind him.

The answer was not what Quillon expected. "Protection, from what?"

"From you, of course," said Elliott as his chair wheeled around where Quillon could see. A pair of dark suited security flanked him, and a man in a white jacket, who took a seat at the video console.

Quillon recognized him from his dream. There was little resemblance to the man in the picture in Georges' office. Same eyes, but the ones that studied him now made him nervous. Without thinking, he said, "I know you."

"And we are going to get to know each other a lot better," said Elliot as he positioned his chair so Quillon could see him without straining.

"I don't think I want to know you better," said Quillon.

"A sense of humor," said Elliott with a smile. "That's important in stressful times like this."

"Look, I did what they asked me to do. I made the portal go away. I think you should let me go, like Professor Georges promised."

"You're a very lucky man," said Elliott, ignoring Quillon's request. "We have spent the past two days discussing what to do about you and thanks to your latest achievement," Elliott stressed the word achievement, then continued, "we have found a reason to let you live a little longer."

Quillon stared at Elliott as his threat worked its way to his stomach. He felt a shiver. Then something else Elliott had said caught his attention. "Two days," said Quillon. "I have been like this for two days! Let me go now or you will regret it."

"Now you see why you are restrained," said Elliott. "You're a very dangerous man. I've watched your performance and I will not let you repeat that spell you used to move the portal. I would also point out that my companions are armed."

Quillon looked at the men in suits and knew he was telling the truth. It was Elliott's comment about a spell that confused him. "What are you talking about?" he asked.

"Don't play dumb with me," said Elliott. "It's insulting and wastes the valuable time you have left."

Quillon could see that Elliot was getting agitated and remembered Georges' warning about not getting him angry. "I'm sorry, but I'm not sure what you're talking about."

Elliott raised his hand slightly and the technician at the video console punched a few buttons and a nearby monitor lit up, showing his room. The portal was still where he left it. The only change was the large red stain on the floor below it. Quillon's heart sank. He had hoped he could leave before it was discovered. "You found it," was all he could say.

"Correct," said Elliot. "Or, to be more accurate, two guards, station in the hallway outside your room, discovered it. They investigated a sound and I think you can guess the rest. Fortunately, the size of the portal still restricted the creature from crossing over."

"I didn't want anyone to get hurt," Quillon said, focusing on the red stain. "I was scared and thought it was going to attack me. The next thing I knew, it was in my room."

"Your ability to move that portal has made you valuable again," said Elliot.

"Look, I promise. I don't know how it got there," said Quillon.

Elliott signaled to the technician again, pointed back to the monitor, and Quillon's eyes followed. There on the screen was Quillon sitting outside the library, slightly slumped over, box in one hand and the other raised high with the dagger held tightly in it. The camera view was from behind him, but Quillon recognized it as the moments shortly before the portal moved. He watched as his fisted hand moved the dagger slowly and awkwardly in small circles, then dropped to his lap the moment the portal vanished. He knew it was Henrietta that moved his hand, but he did not see any trace of her on the screen.

"There!" said Elliott as he reversed and replayed the scene. "That is the spell you are going to teach me."

"You're mistaken," said Quillon as Elliott had the scene replayed over and over. "I didn't do that. It was my sister."

"Doctor Taylor could not prove the existence of your sister. That trick may have worked on Georges, but it won't work on me," said Elliott.

"Honest," said Quillon. "It's hard to explain, but I was inside the creature looking at myself at that moment and it was my sister that was moving my arm. I could feel the creature getting upset and was sure it was going to attack. I did my best to hold it back, but felt like I was losing control. I thought about how much I wanted to be somewhere else." Quillon paused for a second then added, "And then I was. After that, I was back in my body, sitting outside the library."

Elliot moved his chair back a few feet and studied Quillon for a few minutes. "Now, that's interesting," said Elliot. He turned to the tech and said, "Pull up the video of his room at the point where the portal appears."

I knew they were watching me, Quillon thought. *I really can't trust anyone in this place.*

"There," said Elliot, and the screen froze. "Take it back a few seconds and play it."

They all watched as the portal popped into Quillon's room. It was much smaller than before. After a few seconds, tentacles extended out of the portal and pressed up against the room's door. Next, the tentacles wandered around the room, as if they were inspecting the area.

"You said you were in your room. Do you remember doing that?" asked Elliot.

Quillon nodded, "I remember wanting to hit the door, and that's when I saw the tentacles touching it."

"Well, you're full of surprises," said Elliot. "Not only can you move the portal, but you exhibited some level of control over the creature. You may have just made your life worth saving."

"If I'm so valuable, do you think I can be treated a little better? Maybe release me?" asked Quillon.

Elliot laughed and said, "Valuable yes, safe no." He signaled to the person behind Quillon, then said, "We will talk again. I have big plans for you. For now, night, night."

Quillon saw a hand adjust something on the IV and once again, the world went black.

Chapter 25
New Understanding

Georges stared at the photos and notes spread out across his desk. The Necro Box, and its contents, sat to one side, placed on top an open file folder full of strange drawings. He leaned back in his chair and rubbed his eyes. Georges had been studying the notes from the Surowiecki files all morning and was feeling the strain. He took a deep breath and let it out, slowly changing his attention to the large monitor and its display of Quillon's room and its new inhabitant.

He squinted a few times, let out a sigh. The view of the portal was not as good as when it was in the library, and the longer he stared at it, the more it bothered him. He buzzed Hayward, who stepped in, tablet in hand.

"Yes, Grand Master. What can I do for you?"

Georges pointed to the screen and said, "I don't like the new angle on the portal. Have maintenance do something about it."

"But the creature is in there, sir. I'm not sure if they can do anything without going in."

"I thought all our cameras moved," said Georges. "Never mind. I want the shot improved. It's their fault if they didn't put in the right camera. Have them get on it right away."

"Yes, sir. Is there anything else?"

"No, that's all," said Georges, as he returned his attention to the papers on his desk, trying to work up the energy to return to his work.

As Hayward was leaving, Yuri tapped on the door and said, "Anyone home?"

Georges stood, pointed to a chair, and said, "Yuri, what a nice and timely interruption. Have a seat. I could use a little pleasant conversation."

"I would love to talk, Ian, but I'm just on my way up to help Elliott get ready for his attempt to contain the portal. I just stopped by to see if you want to accompany me."

"I'm not going," said Georges, glancing back at his desk. He continued, "Too much to do here." As he returned to his chair, he said, "Stay, I will make it worth your while."

Yuri stepped up to the closest chair and placed his hands on the seat back and said, "I can't stay. It appears I have a part to play in his plans"

Georges let out a soft chuckle of disgust, shaking his head slightly. "Well, I guess they needed someone nearby who could put out any fires he started."

"No, he just wants someone to convince Quillon to assist him with his plan."

"You mean someone with a kinder, gentler face?" said Georges with a smirk.

"He thinks I can talk Quillon into moving the portal into the summoning circle in the Grand Ceremonial Theater," said Yuri.

"Take my advice. Don't be anywhere near the place once the experiment starts," said Georges, gathering the pictures in front of him into a pile.

"You seem to have little confidence in Elliott succeeding."

"What I'm saying is that Elliott is so clouded with his hatred for me and desire to prove himself that he has made the same mistake all self-proclaimed experts make. They see everything through the lens of their past successes," said Georges, leaning back in his chair. "He won't admit that this is something very ancient, very dangerous. Something whose true nature is only glimpsed at in the Surowiecki papers."

"Are you suggesting that he is doing something wrong? Something that could be harmful to those involved?" Leaning forward, Yuri continued, "If so, it is your duty as the Grand Master to intervene."

Georges chuckled, then said, "He wouldn't listen if I said something. I have asked Stephanus to be prepared just in case, and I'm advising you not to get involved."

Yuri rubbed his chin while he studied Georges. He could see the stress on his old friend's face. "You're probably right about him not listening to you. Do you want me to try?"

"He will just point out that you have less understanding of what he does than I do," said Georges. "I think the best thing we can do is prepare for what we do next."

Yuri glanced at the items on Georges' desk and said, I'm guessing that has something to do with the Necro Box."

Georges did not answer for a few minutes. Instead, he rummaged through the papers on his desk. He collected a few photos and placed them on the edge of the desk nearest to Yuri and said, "Have a look at these."

Yuri picked up the photos, glanced at them quickly, then returned them to the desk edge. "Quillon's tattoos," he said. "What of it?"

Georges picked up the book of drawings and handed it to Yuri.

"What are these?" Yuri asked as he flipped the pages.

"When we first met with Elliott on this project, he commented on tattoos being used to assist or protect during a summoning. This shows a collection of known symbols used in the manner Elliott suggested."

"I remember," said Yuri, handing the book back to Georges. "None of those looked like the pictures of Quillon's tattoo."

"Exactly," said Georges, smiling as he returned the book to its place under the box. "All the examples in that book are simple. There is nothing as complicated as Quillon's tattoo." Georges reached for the box and placed it on the edge of the desk and said, "The designs on the Necro Box are the only things I've found that look like Quillon's tattoos."

Yuri retrieved the photos of Quillon's tattoo and compared them to the pattern on the box. After a few minutes, he returned the photos to the desk. "Interesting," he said. "But what does it have to do with what Elliott is doing?"

"As the Grand Master, I'm expected to have a basic understanding of all the areas under our authority. I may not have Elliott's expertise in summoning, but I have some understanding. When we first met on this project, Elliot gave his impression of what was going on, including comments on the marking on Quillon, simple as they were at the time. After we had our disagreement, I must admit I was too proud and worried about my honor to let anyone see my weaknesses in the area of summoning. I accepted what our expert said and ran with it. I had a nagging suspicion that there was something else going on and Doctor Taylor gave me the only avenue to investigate it."

"You told me she left because it had nothing to do with her area of study."

"She left because she was scared," said Georges. "Because something unnatural was involved. Remember, she said magic was used to capture the soul of a person in the Necro Box."

"So, you think it's alive?" That it's working magic of some kind?" asked Yuri, looking at the box sitting just a few feet from him.

"I'm not ready to go that far," said Georges, "but it's clear in the video I watched, Quillon was under some kind of influence," said Georges. "I found it interesting the way the tattoo reacted to the dagger. It climbed his arm almost like it was trying to reach it."

"What then?" asked Yuri. "Is he turning into another box?"

Georges stared at Yuri for several seconds, then a smile grew on his face as a new and interesting idea came to him.

Yuri saw Georges was deep in thought and he was thinking of what to say next when Hayward knocked on the door and stepped in.

"I'm sorry to interrupt, Grand Master. I spoke with maintenance. They are going to see if it is possible to drill a hole in the wall for a new camera or maybe send in a robot."

Georges thanked him and then said to Yuri, "They are getting me a better angle of the portal."

Yuri smiled and said, "You might hold off on that. If Elliott is successful, it won't be there much longer."

Georges looked up at the monitor, surprised that he hadn't thought of that. He looked over to Hayward, who was still waiting by the door and told him to have maintenance hold off on making in chances for a day. Hayward nodded but did not leave. "Is there something else?"

"There are two security officers here. They have instructions from Regent Elliott to pick up the Necro Box and dagger and take it to him."

Yuri smiled and said, "Maybe Elliot has rethought things."

Georges picked up the box and reluctantly offered it to Hayward.

"I wonder what he is going to do with that?" Georges asked, almost to himself.

"You can always come with me and find out," said Yuri as he headed for the door.

"No, like I said, I want to give Elliott all the room he needs, and I would appreciate it if you didn't mention our talk."

"Of course." said Yuri. "I have kept your secrets in the past, and I promise I will tell no one about what we said here."

"Thank you, Yuri. You're a good friend," said Georges.

Yuri gave a slight wave, and as the door closed behind him, Georges looked at the pile of papers and photos spread out on his desk. He picked up a photo of Quillon's tattoo and said, with a chuckle, "Another box. That's a very interesting idea."

Chapter 26
Trip to the Zoo

When Quillon woke up this time, he saw the face of another stranger. He was a little taken aback because this one was smiling at him. Quillon's eyes itched and his vision was a little blurry. He rubbed them and things were clearer. That's when he realized he was no longer restrained. He looked at his arm and the IV was gone. A quick check revealed that he was no longer hooked to anything.

"My name is Yuri," said the stranger, still smiling. "I'm a friend of Professor Georges."

"Is he here?" asked Quillon, looking around. He was disappointed to find that he was still in the control room. "Where is he? Does he know what's happening to me?"

"He does now, and he asked me to check on you," said Yuri as he stepped aside while a person in a lab coat directed a strange looking electric wheelchair into the room. "Why don't you have a seat, and we'll have a little walk and discuss things?"

It surprised Quillon how weak he was. He needed help to get to the wheelchair. Once seated, he could get a better view of the control room and the gurney he had spent an unknown amount of time on. The room was a good size room, large enough for the three technicians, and twice as many security to move around without stepping on each other. "Where's Elliot?" he asked.

"That would be Regent Elliot to you. He is very touchy about how he is addressed," said Yuri with a slight smile, as he stepped behind Quillon and took hold of the chair handles.

"Right, I wouldn't want to get on his bad side," said Quillon.

The chair made a soft whirring sound as it was turned around. Quillon looked around but did not see any controls for him to use. "High Tech," said Quillon. "I hope Regent Elliot won't mind me using his equipment."

"I would be careful not to mention his wheelchair. He is a little touchy about that too," said Yuri. "He came by it later in his life. Not all the events conducted here are safe. Besides, being a man of action, you will never see him using an electric one."

"Where are we going?" asked Quillon as Yuri directed the chair through the door of the control room and into a hallway with an elevator and two frosted doors at either end. When Yuri turned the wheelchair to face one of the doors, Quillon became concerned again. "I thought we were going down."

"Down you know. Something much more interesting waits on the other side of this door," said Yuri, as he pressed a metal plate with a blue wheelchair symbol on the wall.

The frosted door opened to reveal a large, circular, well lit, beautiful space. It looked almost like the center court of a mall or the lobby of some grand hotel.

The ceiling had to be twenty feet up. The gold-colored walls were covered with large back lit, colorful pictures of people and events, each mixed in with strange writing.

The floor was a light golden granite with various inlays with different shades of light and dark gold. It had two large circles made of bright golden inlay. One circle bordered the edge of the room, just inside the many columns that marked its border. A second golden circle marked the boundaries of a circular platform set in the center of the room. It was raised about six inches from the floor, with small blue LED lights showing every few feet.

Above the platform, the ceiling had a matching circle. Inside was a large circular skylight made from brightly colored glass, with a center that dropped down about three feet, forming an upside-down pyramid.

Extending from the outer edge of the ceiling circle were beams that traveled out like rays toward the walls.

Spaced around the inner circle were smaller circles, like Quillon had seen in his dream. Above each small circle was a beautiful art déco lamp hung on long poles. Inside each of these smaller circles were strange symbols, set in a jet-black stone.

Quillon was speechless. This room was completely out of character with the design of the building he had spent the past few days in. He almost felt that he had been transported to another place and time.

"Amazing, isn't it?" said Yuri. "I love this place. I could spend hours here."

"What is it?" said Quillon, still trying to take it all in.

"This is our Grand Ceremonial Theater," said Yuri. "We do our most dangerous work here. This is where your portal should have been summoned. It does not look like it, but they designed this space from the floor up to handle something like that. We also have another space, through the other set of doors near the elevator, where dangerous items like that box and its dagger are supposed to be tucked safely away. You should have never been exposed to it, and I, for one, am truly sorry for what has happened to you."

The apology left Quillon as silent as the room they were in. It was something that he had wanted, and now that he got it, he was surprised how much it impacted him. He could feel the emotion welling up inside. The most he could manage was a weak "Thanks, that means a lot."

"Back to our tour," said Yuri as he continued to push Quillon around the room. "I don't know if Regent Elliot has let you in on what he has planned for you."

"He told me nothing. I was hoping you were here to rescue me from him."

Yuri stopped in one of the smaller circles at the far end of the room. He put Quillon in the center. Then turned the chair so he could see both the windows of the control room and the door they had entered through. Quillon heard a beep from the wheelchair. "That's the brakes. Don't want you missing this view," said Yuri as he stepped beside Quillon.

"You might not believe this, but both Regent Elliot and Grand Master Georges want the same thing; mastery of the portal and the creature within. However, they have very different ideas on how to go about it."

"Then why am I here?" asked Quillon, testing the brakes. "Take me to Professor Georges, and we can try something else. I really don't like dealing with Regent Elliott."

"The brakes are electronic, and very strong," said Yuri, turning toward Quillon. "Unfortunately, the Board of Regents has backed Regent Elliot. They were quick to remind the Grand Master that he started this. They also consider your attempt, tho revealing, to be short of what he promised. Regent Elliott was told to proceed with his ideas on how to control the creature."

"I would be more than happy to let him go play with the creature. Just leave me out of it."

Yuri chuckled, then said, "I'm sure he would love to do that, but the creature does not want to play with him. You seem to be the only one that can get the creature and the portal to do what is required."

"If you're talking about my moving the portal, I already told Regent Elliot that I'm not sure how that happened."

"I believe you," said Yuri. "We have done some wild and crazy brainstorming and are convinced that the instructions to move were emotion driven. Done in the heat of panic. As for where you moved it, best we can figure is that you can only move it to someplace that you're emotionally attached to."

"If that is so, it proves what I told everyone. I didn't know what I was doing when I did it."

"Like I said. I believe you. Now, down to business." Yuri took a few steps toward the center platform, turned, and said, "See the large circle in the center? That is the next place the portal is going to call home. It will be your job to put it there. Somewhere we can finally control it."

"I still don't really know how to get it there."

"We have some ideas about that. First, I want you to get to know the place. We are going to let you sit here for a while and take in the view. Focus on the circle and think of it like your room, only fancier."

"And after the portal is trapped there, I can leave, right?" asked Quillon.

Yuri did not answer at first, but continued to look around the room. Still looking away from Quillon he said, "When I was a small boy, my father would take me to the zoo." Yuri paused, as if remembering something, then turned toward Quillon as he asked, "Have you ever been to the zoo?"

"Sure," said Quillon, not sure what he was getting at.

"I loved it. A very exciting place for a small child," said Yuri as he made his way behind Quillon again and placed his hands on the handles of the wheelchair. "As I got older, I read about how bad it was to keep animals in places like a zoo. Away from their natural environment. People said an animal is not an animal if it is not in the wild. Since I came from a rich family, I became quite the activist, and was successful in getting many places shut down and the animals released. As I got older, I came to understand that habitats like zoos were the only place where certain animals could exist. It was a place where they could be properly cared for and protected. A place where endangered animals could live out their lives safely."

"That's a nice story," said Quillon. "But it does not answer my question."

"I'm sorry, Quillon, but you're one of those endangered animals. As long as those fragments are in you, and the portal exists, you cannot leave. It is for both your safety and for the safety of others. The problem for me now is making sure you have the best zookeeper taking care of you."

"I'm not an animal," said Quillon. He tried to move the wheelchair, but the locks prevented him.

"Look around. You'll see the way we came is the only exit. Those people waiting there see you as someone they need to contain." Yuri let out a sigh and continued, "I can guarantee they are very good at their job."

Quillon could see three of the dark suited security. He knew those suit jackets hid something more powerful than a taser.

"I want you to sit here for about fifteen minutes and focus on that circle. Your future depends on you putting that portal there."

"How am I supposed to have happy thoughts about that circle after everything you have told me?"

"I never said the emotions associated with where you sent the portal needed to be happy. I think you sent the thing to your room because it had a locking door. Just keep that thought in your head and remember, that circle has the kind of lock needed for the portal."

Quillon hadn't thought about why the portal ended up in his room, but that suggestion made a lot of sense.

"As far as zookeepers," said Yuri, stepping beside the chair placing a hand on Quillon's shoulder, "Who knows? If certain things keep going the way I think they are going, I may end up being your zookeeper. If that happens, I will do my best to make your stay a happy one."

Quillon watched Yuri walk away and with him his hope of finding someone that would help him. He realized Georges would not come to his aid. *I ought to drop that portal right in his office. Let him figure out how to close it,* he thought with a chuckle. His good humor quickly vanished when the surrounding reminded him who he was dealing with and how little hope he had of escaping without doing what they asked. The only ray of hope he had was Jackson's words to trust his sister. "Ok Henrietta," said Quillon quietly as he watched the security that was watching him. "Let's give them what they want, then you're going to help me get out of here no matter who gets hurt."

Chapter 27
Please Henrietta

Quillon nibbled at the little sandwiches they had brought for him. He never understood why anyone would cut the crust off. He liked the feel of crust on a sandwich. It let him know that what was inside would not fall out. Plus, these trimmed sandwiches always felt a little drier than normal. He opened the bread to look at the thin spread inside, then took a few more bites. His stomach hurt and he wondered how long it had been since he ate, but was not in a talkative mood. The time he had spent in the wheelchair helped him gain back some of his strength. He could even walk back to the control room.

The two technicians were busy adjusting the video presentations on the large screens and the three taser armed security officers were doing their best at being invisible, which made them stand out to Quillon even more.

Quillon almost choked on his sandwich when two of the video monitors changed from the test pattern to his room. There was the portal, still floating over the bloodstained floor. It appeared a little smaller than he remembered.

The other two monitors displayed the room outside the control room. One was a wide shot, and the other zoomed in on what everyone hoped would be the new resting place for the portal.

As if on cue, the elevator chimed, and Quillon turned to see the door open, showing a crowded elevator. He could see Elliot waiting in the back, as three dark suited security men and what looked like two medical personnel exited before him.

Professor Georges and Yuri had both said that Elliot had acted out of concern for both Quillon and others. All that talk meant nothing, now that he was facing him again. Each meeting with him, either in his dreams or in person, were filled with death or violence. To Quillon, the man was a bully. He said little, but the people with him responded quickly. He could not imagine what it would be like working for someone like him.

Elliot wheeled himself to the far end of the control room. He put on some dark gloves as one of his men took a small case from the back of his chair and opened it for him. Elliot reached in and pulled out the Necro Box.

Quillon had felt it arrive and knew that the dagger rested inside.

Elliot smiled when he saw Quillon's eyes fixed on the box. "Beautiful, isn't it?" he said. "Since access to it was forbidden, even to me, I never really got the chance to study it." As he lifted it up and studied the pattern. Glancing at Quillon, he said, "It's clear that you have deeper understanding of their purpose. Maybe we can compare notes when this is all done."

Quillon could see the smirk on Elliott's face and said, "It's easy. Just stab yourself with the dagger. The rest just happens."

Elliott gave Quillon a smile as he opened the box, revealing the dagger inside. Quillon could feel his heart beating faster and the portal on the monitor flicked a bit and seem to grow as if waking up. Quillon was not the only one to see the reaction.

"So, it is true, you are linked to the portal," said Elliott with a sense of satisfaction. "That means our experiment should have the outcome we all are hoping for." Elliot raised his hand then said, "But first, we need to get you ready."

The two medical people Quillon had seen getting off the elevators stepped forward. One pushing the wheelchair Quillon had used earlier. They had added a post to it.

"What's this? Don't think I'm going to let you put me back under. I will fight you if you do!" said Quillon, standing up. He still felt weak, but did his best to appear steady.

"This is for your blood transfusion," said one of the medical personnel, pointing to the wheelchair where the other medical tech was hanging a bag of blood.

"Are you sure you want to do this? I had a bad experience the last time," said Quillon.

"We need you at your best. Besides, I can't have you passing out halfway through the experiment," said Elliot. When Quillon did not move, Elliot raised his hand and the three security men stepped forward. "Like I said, this is for your own good. Please don't make us force you to do what is needed."

"For my good," said Quillon, as he looked around. "Where have I heard that before?" He sighed and made his way to the chair. "No restraints this time!" he said to the person helping him into the chair.

"I don't think that will be necessary," said Elliot.

"What do you want me to do?" asked Quillon as he stared at the box.

"Simple. Move the portal into the circle as you were instructed," said Elliot, pointing from the monitor with his room on it to the monitor of the platform in the summoning theater. "We also have some interest in seeing how much control you have over the creature within the portal."

Quillon felt the pinch of the needle as it entered his arm and said, "I have told you and Yuri that I'm not sure I can do that. I know I did it before, but I'm not sure how I did it."

"Yes, so you have said. However, I think I know how to deal with that. We are going to let you try it on your own first. If not, we will explore another approach."

Quillon felt a bracelet being attached to his wrist. "What's this?" he asked. "I said no restraints."

"It's nothing like that," said Elliot. "My reports show that you have," he paused, then continued, "difficulties in breaking your link with the creature."

Quillon's silence encouraged Elliott. "I thought so," he said with a smile. "Doctor Taylor had some interesting thoughts about that."

The man who attached the bracelet handed Elliott a small box and stepped behind Quillon, out of his sight.

"We are concerned that the deeper the link, the harder it will be for you to break it," said Elliot as he held up the small control and pressed it. Quillon got a mild shock, which caused his hand to shake. It felt as if his arm had gone numb for a few seconds. "See, no actual damage. It works kind of like a baby taser. Just enough of a message to get you back to our side of things."

Quillon reached for the bracelet, and Elliott pressed the button again. The shock caused Quillon to pull his hand back.

"Now that we understand that, I think it's time to get on with this experiment."

Elliot rolled closer to Quillon and held the box out toward him. "Take it. We are not sure if you will hear us once you link with the creature. We will also use the intercom in your room to give you instructions. Your job is simple. Move the portal and we will be done."

Quillon took the box, and as he placed it in his lap, he could feel the blood flow through his veins as the transfusion began. As he stared at the box, the patterns started to slowly move. He closed his eyes, preparing for what he worried would come next.

Instead, Quillon felt good, as if he was getting strength from somewhere else. He felt the tattoo across his chest warming as well, but that soon became only a minor irritation.

When he opened his eyes, he was in his old room. The smell of old blood and bits of decaying flesh assaulted his nose. They had turned the ventilation off and the room was warm, almost hot. He guessed that some of the smell and environment were spilling over from the side of the portal he now viewed the room through.

"Quillon, can you hear us?" came Elliot's voice through the intercom. It sounded strange, but he could still understand it. He tried to say something, but the sound that came out sounded like a wild animal.

"Quillon, if you can hear us, please signal."

Thinking back to the encounter he had with the security in the library, Quillon tried moving his arms, hoping to show he understood. He felt his body stir and watched as long, thick tentacles extended into the room. He did his best to move all of them in a waving fashion, not sure how to control each tentacle individually.

"Okay, we see you," said the intercom. "If that's you, stop moving."

Quillon complied, and the intercom said, "Good. Now move the portal inside the circle in the middle of the grand ceremonial theater."

Moving the creature became easier. The more he did it, the less he felt like he was a puppet master, and more like a man wearing a suit. But try as he could, he could not get the portal to budge. It had grown larger, and it took a lot of effort to keep the creature from squeezing through.

The more Quillon worked at it, the more tired he got. He could feel his control on the beast slipping. It almost relieved him when he heard the intercom say, "This is not working. Time to try something different."

Quillon hoped that meant the experiment would end soon. He did not see the problem with just keeping the portal here. It seemed to be a safe place for now. That circle upstairs was out in the open, no doors or walls to keep it in.

The intercom said, "I have been told you may need some emotional motivation to move the portal. I'm going to give you a choice. A very simple choice. One between life and death."

With that, the door to the room opened and two men tossed something that looked like a body into the room.

When it turned over, Quillon could see it was a woman. She appeared old and disheveled. She reminded him of the street people he had seen so often in his old neighborhood. A few had snuck into the warehouse where he worked, looking for someplace warm to sleep. He had hated calling the police on them, but that was what he got paid for.

As he studied the woman, he realized there was something strange in the way she just laid there, almost like she did not know what was going on. *She has to be drugged,* he thought. He got a quick whiff of urine mixed with something else. When the woman looked up, he saw her face was swollen where she had been beaten. There was also a trickle of blood around her mouth and nose.

Seeing the blood and the condition of her face brought both a feeling of anger mixed with the grumble of hunger. He stared into her face, not sure if she could understand the danger that stirred just feet from her.

Over sounds of the stirring behind him, Quillon heard the intercom say, "Move the portal and she lives. Control the beast and she lives, but for how long? Your choice."

Quillon roared with anger. The woman on the floor drifted in and out of consciousness. However, his scream of anger had gotten her attention. She struggled to crawl away from the source. He could see her eyes now open wide in terror as an understanding of the danger she was in made its way through the drugs.

A pain in his chest and a widening of his view of the room told him the portal was drawing more blood. He could feel the fatigue of holding himself back. The cracks in his control were showing, as he had to struggle to pull back the increasing numbers of tentacles reaching out before him. Some had reached the woman and batted her around like a toy, but he refused to let them grab hold. He was not sure how much longer he could hold out. He needed to move the portal if he was going to save her.

Quillon focused on the slight tightness he felt across his chest. He knew that feeling came from his connection to the portal. Focusing on the portal and controlling the creature was becoming almost impossible. His chest pounded, and he could feel the portal in-sync. He was doing it, but he could see that one of his arms had wrapped itself around the woman's legs and was pulling her toward the portal.

Quillon was not sure if she was still alive, but he would not watch as it devoured her in front of him. He put his mind back into moving the portal when suddenly he felt a strange tingling sensation and felt himself slipping from the mind of the creature.

It took a few seconds for Quillon to understand what had happened. Elliot had used the shocking bracelet to bring him back. He looked up to see the control room and there on the monitors he saw his room. Empty now except for the new blood stains and what looked like the remains of the woman being pulled into the void.

"Why did you do that? I stopped the creature from killing her! A few more seconds and I would have moved the portal!"

"Her death was your fault," said Elliot calmly. "I gave you a choice, and you picked the one that led to her death."

"She died because you did nothing!" said Quillon. "You could have saved her. You saw I was holding back the creature."

"She was not worth saving, and her habit was going to kill her soon or later. This way, her death served the greater good."

Quillon did not know what to say. He realized he was looking at a bigger monster than the one inside the portal. The only thing he could think to say was, "I did what you asked. I proved I can control the beast. Now let me go."

"Yes, you have proved what we already guessed. The holder of the dagger can control the creature. As exciting as that is, your real value, the reason for you to stay alive, depends on putting the portal in the circle. Once again, the choice is yours. Do it, or someone else will die," Elliot paused, then said, "The streets offer an almost endless supply of motivation."

Quillon stared at Elliot. His eyes tightened in anger, and the tightness in his chest grew. He looked down at the dagger in his hands, closed his eyes, and when he opened them, he was looking at Elliot again, but from behind him. Through the frame of the portal window, he also saw himself and the frightened looks of the technicians and security around him.

Elliott slowly turned his chair to face the portal behind him. Quillon could see the fear edging in panic in Elliot's eyes as he looked up into the eyes Quillon now used to look back.

Quillon tried to say something, but the sound that came out was chilling and did nothing to calm the anger he felt at Elliot, which now boiled out of him, just like the increasing number of tentacles that poured out of the portal.

Elliot soon disappeared in a bundle of tentacles, which dragged him back into the portal before he had time to scream. When a sound came, it was behind Quillon. A muffled cry among other unworldly sounds.

Quillon heard gunfire, but felt little of the pain he was sure it caused. He returned his attention to the source of gunfire. There, in front of him, stood one of the dark suited security officers, gun drawn, and pointed toward the thing in the portal. Next to him, Quillon saw himself, still sitting in the wheelchair, holding the box and dagger.

There was the ding of the elevator door. The technicians and the taser armed security that were already clustered in the hallway, piled in. To their credit, the dark suited security men had stood their ground, weapons drawn.

Several tentacles made their way slowly back into the control room. They lay on the control room floor, waiting for Quillon's next instructions.

Quillon watched as the gun held by the closest man shifted its aim from the portal to the helpless version of himself sitting in the wheelchair. When the others did the same, Quillon panicked, and in that moment, he felt uncontrollable anger filling his mind. He could not control himself as he lashed out toward the threat.

The force of the tentacles smashed one man against the wall, killing him. Other tentacles snapped at the two remaining men like a whip, knocking them to the floor. Quillon saw a tentacle grab one of the downed men and lift him into the air. The elevator opened again, and the other fallen man scrambled across the floor towards it. Quillon reached for him. The man shot at the gray arm holding the doors open. Quillon winced at the pain and pulled the arm back, dragging most of the man back with it.

With the last man being ravished by tentacles, Quillon felt the anger leaving. It was then that Quillon realized he didn't have control over several of the arms moving about the control room, including those he saw making their way slowly toward him. He needed to do something quick if he did not want to join Elliot.

Through the window of the control room, Quillon could see the little platform in the center of the summoning theater. His very life depended on him moving the portal there. Quillon struggled to pull his arms back into the portal.

He thought back to his view of the circle from where Yuri left him, and just willed with all his might for the portal to be there. He felt the warmth of the connection and saw the flash just before he felt a pain in his head, like he had run into a wall headfirst.

Quillon opened his eyes, and he was sitting in the wheelchair looking at an empty spot where the portal had been seconds ago. He looked around and saw a grizzly sight. The surrounding carpet was blood soaked, and the walls and floor were splattered with the remains of both creature and man. When the portal moved, it must have cut off some tentacles sticking through it. As for the security men, what happened there was obvious.

Quillon's head hurt and he was weak, but he unhooked himself and stood to see if he had been successful. He heard the box and dagger hit the ground as he stood. The view of his efforts left him stunned.

The portal was in the golden room, but it was not on the platform. Instead, it floated just on the outer edge of the circle that surrounded the platform. Nothing had exited, so he guessed the pain of the experience of the move dampened the hunger of the waiting beast. Quillon knew that would not last long.

The ding of the elevator surprised Quillon. He turned to see Stephanus and five others exit, guns drawn. Stephanus directed his men towards the summoning theater before stopping at the control doorway and shouting, "Put it in the circle!"

"I can't. Something is stopping me." The sound of gunfire drew his attention back to the portal, where he saw several tentacles struggling to exit. He felt a pain in his chest and could see the portal widening larger. He wondered how much wider could it get without killing him.

The sound of gunfire halted as Stephanus's men came stumbling into the control room. Stephanus followed, dragging one of his men. As he stepped through the mess of mutilated bodies, he looked around and said, "How did this happen?" Before Quillon could respond, he said, "Never mind!" He fired a few shots into the windows, shattering them. "If you can't move it to the circle, move it someplace else."

Quillon had reached the same idea a few seconds before Stephanus said it. He glanced through the control room window again and was shocked by what he saw.

The portal was larger now than when he moved it a few minutes ago. The pain in his chest was less now, but it continued somehow to grow. It had almost reached the ceiling and he could see the creature pushing its way through the ever-enlarging opening.

How am I supposed to move something that big? he asked himself, sliding back down to the floor, his back against the control panel. He felt like it had taken all his energy to move it to where it now sat. Another thought struck him, *Where am I going to move it too? It's too big for the library or my room.*

That's when he saw the dagger lying in a pool of blood. It took him a few seconds to realize that the blade was absorbing the blood it sat in, fueling the growth of the portal.

Quillon quickly grabbed the blade, wiped the blood on his shirt and searched around for the box, which he found next to an arm. He grabbed it and stuffed the dagger inside just as three more security officers exited the elevator.

Stephanus shouted, "One of you, take the door, the rest join me." As one of the officers entered the control room, he signaled for Quillon to move so he could take his place near the window. Quillon nodded and made a dash for the elevator, the box and its contents in his hand, hoping to catch it before it closed, but was just seconds too late. He stood, head leaning against the elevator doors, knowing that he did not have the card needed to open it.

There was a tremendous noise, and shattering glass from the nearby door caused him to jump back just in time to escape the large tentacle as it slammed onto the ground. It quickly retreated through the shattered frosted door, dragging a screaming man who did his best to fire his gun at the beast. His screaming and the gunfire were short-lived.

Quillon stood paralyzed in those few seconds, but the shadows of more tentacles brought him to his senses and he made his way back into the control room. He sat terrified, knees to his chest, the box on his lap and his hands around his ears, doing his best to block out the sounds of gunfire and yelling.

Quillon heard another crash of glass and guessed it must be the skylight above the small stage where he was supposed to send the portal.

The erratic gunfire, and the look of terror on the men, told Quillon the creature had escaped the portal. Looking at the small group of defenders, he felt helpless. Soon tentacles would be eagerly pouring through the control room windows. The last time he felt this desperate was the day he tried to kill himself. He covered his ears and did his best to block out the sound of chaos and thought about Henrietta.

In the past, in those dreams, she had encouraged him to join her. Now, each time he saw her, the feeling was different. She came with pain, but she also helped end the dreams. The more he thought about it, the more he felt she was helping him. He called out to her now, "Henrietta, please, I am sorry for what happened. Please, I need your help. I don't want to die."

Quillon closed his eyes to fight back the tears. There was another loud scream from the other side of the wall, which brought his attention back to his current situation. That's when he noticed his hands getting warm and his back and chest itched. He looked down at the box he was still holding in his hand and noticed the pattern on it move. It was almost hypnotic. As it moved, he felt the itch on his back spread, followed by pain, which forced him to clutch the box tighter to his chest.

The more his back hurt, the louder the screaming became in the other room. A scream that Quillon understood from his time with the creature was anger. Quillon soon understood it was the box that angered the creature. The box, and somehow Quillon as well. He expected it to smash through the wall at any minute and destroy the thing that was responsible for its anger.

There was a loud crash and the sound of falling debris and Quillon closed his eyes tight and held his breath, waiting for the end. When he could hold his breath no longer, he let it out slowly. Still afraid to look, he sat eyes closed and shaking until he heard someone shout, "What are you doing?"

He opened his eyes and saw Stephanus staring at him. "You were supposed to move it someplace. Not let it get away!" Turning to a nearby officer, he said, "Take him to the Grand Master. The rest of you come with me."

As Quillon stood, he looked through the shattered windows and saw the room cluttered with debris. The portal still floated where he left it, but it was huge, part of it sticking through the roof. *It must have knocked down the roof,* he thought. *It's way too big for me to move.*

Partly visible under the concrete and metal of the fallen roof, he saw the smeared trail of blood that led to the portal and the mangled bodies of maybe two officers partly exposed in the rubble. The one thing he couldn't see was the creature.

Chapter 28
I Don't Want to Know

"We have received calls from the village. The creature is there. We have reports of deaths and lots of damage. I should have drones over it soon," said Stephanus. "I'm having the feed put through to your monitor."

"Fine," said Georges. He leaned back in his chair and peeked into his desk drawer, only to find an empty bottle. He closed the drawer a little harder than he had wanted to. Looking back at Stephanus, whose face gave no sign if he had heard the clinking sound of the empty bottle, and said, "Were you able to put together a team?"

"Yes," said Stephanus, "I have outfitted them with more powerful weapons, but I wish my requests for bigger stuff hadn't been refused."

"We're not the military," said Georges. "The things you asked for would bring us more attention than anything we deal with here."

"Are you suggesting that our current problem will not get noticed?" asked Yuri.

Quillon sat staring at the tattoo on his arm, not really following the conversation. Shortly after being brought to Georges' office, he was asked to link with the creature so they could locate it. Quillon tried several times without success and was thankful when Stephanus arrived with his news about the village.

Stephanus touched the receiver in his ear, and a few seconds later he said, "Understood. Put it through."

The monitor flickered, and the screen filled with a bird's eye view of the creature sitting partly inside the corner of a crumbling building. It was clear that the creature caused the wreckage. At first glance, the reason for it entering the building wasn't clear, but the evidence of blood stains suggested it had followed or chased someone into the building.

"My God! It's huge," said Quillon. "I saw it in my dream, but never for real." He sat staring at the monitor. A look of panic growing on his face. "I'm not going anywhere near that thing. Look at it!"

"Be quiet!" said Georges. "People are dead because you didn't do what you were told. You will face it again. Stephanus will make sure of that, no matter what he needs to do."

Quillon was taken aback by the anger in Georges' voice and worried about the smirk on Stephanus' face.

"I recognize that place," said Yuri, leaning forward. "It's the grocery store. I have only been there a few times. I hate to think of the damage it did to get this far into the downtown."

As they were watching, a group of three people darted from one of the nearby doorways. The waving tentacles instantly caught two up, almost like the thing had been waiting.

The other, a small child, hid, crouched down behind a car. The creature seemed content with devouring the two it grabbed. Quillon was thankful he could not hear the screaming this time.

"We have to do something, or it is going to kill that kid!" said Quillon, as he took several steps toward the monitor. "Is that a park or playground in the background?"

"The elementary school should be the building next to the grocery store," said Georges.

The creature was almost done devouring the two it had snatched up and the smaller tentacles tapped around the area, almost like a dog sniffing for a trail.

"Looks like the kid is next," said Yuri. "Maybe we should focus on moving the portal before a bunch of others get killed."

"I can't stand by and watch that little kid get eaten!" Quillon snatched the box from the desk and headed for the door.

"Where are you going?" asked Georges.

"I need someplace to focus, away from that," said Quillon, pointing toward the monitor. "I'm going to try linking with the thing again."

"Hold on, I have someplace," said Georges, as he walked over to a wall and tapped his card. The panel opened to reveal a bathroom. "Use this. Close the door and you won't be bothered."

Quillon ran into the bathroom, taking one last look at the monitor on his way. He sat on the toilet and started taking deep slow breaths, something his therapist had taught him to deal with anxiety. With the door closed, he had the quiet he needed.

Even though Quillon could not see what was happening, he could not stop seeing the scene of the little boy hiding behind that car while the creature slowly reached out for him. This whole thing was becoming more than he could stand. People had died, and he felt helpless.

Quillon felt anger. He hated the Foundation, but most of all, he hated that creature. Quillon could almost imagine the fear that the little boy felt. He could almost smell it. The fear mixed with the smell of blood and smoke. It was all around him. Quillon glanced at his hands and saw the blood that covered them. Long thin hands on the end of long thin tentacles. A chill ran through his body as he realized what he was looking at. In that moment of stillness, he could smell and hear the traces of chaos mixed with the quiet sound of a small child crying. He also felt the urge to reach out for that sound and quiet it.

"No!" shouted Quillon. At least he thought he shouted it. A shiver ran through his body, followed by a pain in his head. *That's new,* thought Quillon. *You know I'm here. Good, because I will not let you kill that kid.*

The creature reached for the child and Quillon fought back. He pulled on the arms in his mind and flung them to the side, smashing into the building to his right, causing the roof to collapse further.

The creature screamed, and Quillon screamed back. Quillon knew he needed to move the creature some place else before it did more damage to the nearby building. That's when he remembered the playground. If he got the creature out in the open, there was a better chance of keeping it from destroying things. It was probably a better place for the portal to end up as well.

The effort to control the creature consumed his attention so much that he completely lost track of his surroundings, including the child. He could not spare the effort to check on the child. He did not remember any of his tentacles feasting on anything, but he felt the damage they caused as they flailed around, striking the building and surrounding objects.

Quillon could feel the fatigue as he moved toward his target, but was not sure if it was his or the creature's. His head hurt. The new trick of the creature of fighting back was making him nauseous.

Suddenly, he felt the resistance lessen and his movement toward the field increase. He could feel a strong desire to move into the woods on the far edge of the field. *Why are you going there?* Quillon wondered. As he studied the approaching woods, Quillon realized the closely packed trees would hinder any placement of the portal. *You bastard. Can you read my mind?*

The eagerness of the creature to move in the direction Quillon wanted eased some of the pressure of controlling it. That gave him the time to focus on his next step, which was moving the portal. He needed to do that soon. He figured the best place to move it was in front of the creature, hoping the forward movement would bring it close enough to use the portal on it.

Quillon felt the handle of the dagger and felt the connection to the portal almost immediately. The familiar ache in his chest followed by the burning and itching of the tattoo that now covered his chest, back and shoulders. There was also a feeling of excitement he had not felt before. He guessed it had something to do with his desire to connect with it.

He visualized the spot in the field where he wanted the portal to sit. He felt a tingle in his hand and heard the beating of his heart.

Quillon could feel the creature reacting as well. It stopped and Quillon could feel a wince of worry, almost edging on fear coming from it. *That's right, you bastard. I'm coming for you,* he thought. With each second that passed, Quillon could feel the burning and itching of his tattoo increase. Soon it was so strong that it pushed any thought of the portal from his mind and only lessened when he released his hold on the dagger. When he got his breathing back under control, he realized the pain had caused him to lose his link with the creature.

"No!" he shouted. Quillon opened his eyes and saw Henrietta standing before him in the bathroom. It was then that he realized she was the one that said no.

"I need to do this, or people will die."

Henrietta stood motionless, continuing to stare at him. He did not see her lips move, but once again he heard the words "No" in his head.

Quillon closed his eyes to block out the image of Henrietta, but the words "No" constantly rang in his ears until he shouted for her repeatedly to be quiet.

He almost hurt himself when he pushed himself backward at the touch of a hand on his shoulder.

Quillon opened his eyes and saw her silhouetted in the bright light of the open door. He quickly got to his feet and pushed past her into the room beyond.

"What did you do?" This time it was Georges' voice.

"I tried to move the portal," said Quillon, rubbing his forehead. "But Henrietta wouldn't let me." He looked back into the bathroom, expecting to see her there. "She just kept saying no, repeatedly."

"But you linked with the creature," Georges said, looking back at the monitor. "That would explain what happened."

"The kid," said Quillon, as his focus returned to the monitor. "Did he get away?"

"We don't know," said Yuri. "The drones followed the creature when it moved."

"We can always order them to search for the child," said Georges.

"No!"

Quillon's answers surprised the others.

"I could not bear it if he didn't make it." said Quillon as he walked back to the area of the monitor. After studying it for a few seconds, he asked, "What's it doing?"

The creature had stopped just on the far edge of the playground and was just sitting there, tentacles close to its body.

"We were hoping you could tell us what's going on," said Yuri. "You were just inside it."

"Did you do anything to it?" asked Georges.

"No, but it knew what I wanted to do," said Quillon with a yawn. "It took all my energy to get it that far away from the buildings. I was sure it was going to make a dash for the forest. It would have been difficult to get the portal near it if it got inside there."

Stephanus stepped up to study the monitor, then smiled at Quillon's yawn and said, "It's sleeping. You wore it out." The slow rhythmic movement of the beast as it took breaths confirmed what Stephanus said. "Now would be a good time to finish it."

"Quick, move the portal to it, then command it to enter," said Georges.

"I can't move it," said Quillon. "I just tried that, and Henrietta wouldn't let me. My tattoo was hurting like crazy, and she kept yelling no in my head."

"She was preventing you?" Asked Yuri. "That's interesting. I would think, based on your most recent dream, she would have no problem with getting the creature back in the portal. I mean, that's kind of her job."

"And yet, she did not prevent you from linking with the creature," said Georges. "She only had issues with you moving the portal."

"She never prevented me from moving it before," said Quillon.

"Then your answer is someplace in that statement," said Stephanus. "It sounds to me like she was giving you a warning."

"It's almost like she is taking an active hand in how you proceed with an action against the creature," said Georges.

It surprised Quillon when Stephanus walked over and put his hand on Quillon's shoulder. Quillon flinched, expecting Stephanus to hurt him. Instead, Stephanus said, "You're an experienced security officer. Trained to take mental notes of situations so that you can report on them later. I want you to calm yourself and think about the times you moved the portal. Take a few deep breaths first, then go through the events in your mind. See them in the order they happen. Then I want you to tell me what was different about this last attempt."

Stephanus' words had a calming effect on Quillon as he realized that what he said was true and there was something he could do to help the situation.

Quillon thought about those events. Soon his mind filled with memories of the pain, the hate, the anger, and the deaths that followed.

Stephanus responded to the expression on Quillon's face and said, "You need to clear away any emotion. Just see the events like watching a movie. Now take a few deep breaths and start over. Say the steps out loud if it makes it easier."

Quillon did as he said, took several deep breaths, and did his best to remove the emotion from his memory of those events. He spoke the steps as they came to him. When he finished, Stephanus said, "Now. Go over your steps today."

As Quillon rattled off the steps he took today, both he and Stephanus seemed to come to the same understanding, but it was Quillon who said, "The location."

"Of course," said Georges. "In all the other cases, Quillon visited the location. Even though he was in the village via the linkup, he did not really know where he was."

"But why would Henrietta stop me from trying?" asked Quillon. "I still don't understand."

"It's my guess she was protecting us," said Stephanus.

"From what?" asked Quillon.

"I see," said Georges. "Yes, I agree." He looked around the room, then said, "If you had tried to move the portal, most likely you would have moved it here. In its current size, the portal would have probably taken out the roof or even the floor, probably killing us all."

There was a long quiet in the room as the realization of what could've happened sunk in. The group studied the monitor and the sleeping creature.

It was Quillon who spoke first, surprising the other by saying, "The only way to do this is for me to go there, isn't it?"

The others didn't need to say anything for Quillon to know the answer. He stared at the sleeping beast while Stephanus gave instructions to his assault team to gather out front.

Chapter 29
The Merry-Go-Round

The ride through the woods would have been more enjoyable if Quillon didn't have to think about where he was going. The SUV he was riding in was the same one that had brought him to the Foundation. He honestly could not remember how many days ago that was. He was being followed by two more dark SUVs with four armed officers in each.

Quillon was upset that Georges was staying behind, saying this was not a job for magicians. When Quillon commented that there were a lot of magicians in that dream, Georges insisted they only needed them for the initial creation of the box and dagger. His parting words were, "Just do what your sister showed you."

Stephanus sat beside Quillon, sensing his concern said, "Forget about the Grand Master. He would just get in the way. This is work for professionals."

Quillon gave a slight smile and said, "At least someone knows what they're doing."

"That better be you when we get there," said Stephanus as he glanced at the tablet with the drone video. He tapped on the image and expanded the video. "The thing is still laying there, but I don't think it's sleeping."

"It knows we're coming," said Quillon as he watched the forest move past.

"Well, that was to be expected. I wish there was some way to use that link of yours to know what it's planning," said Stephanus. He expanded the image and studied the surroundings. "It's not dumb."

Stephanus showed the image to Quillon and said, "It's waiting on the edge of a forest. It's big, but we could lose it in there if it ran. That clearing space in front of it leaves little cover if we need to get closer. What I wouldn't give for some killer drones about now."

"We could always wait," said Quillon, hopefully. "Maybe one of your buddies could help you out."

"Look closer," said Stephanus, tapping the table. "This is an elementary school. I'm sure there are still people hiding in the surrounding buildings, waiting for help. The Foundation takes care of its own. Georges has called for help from other chapters, but I'm not sure what that would look like, or how long it will take to get here. I could call in some favors, but it would be impossible to keep their help quiet. The last thing we want is for the public to know about us or what we do."

"We are almost there, Director," said the driver. "What are your instructions?"

Stephanus handed Quillon the tablet and said, "Where are you going to put the portal?"

"I hadn't really thought about that," said Quillon as his stomach grumbled.

"How far was it from the creature in your dream?" asked Stephanus.

"About fifteen or twenty feet, I guess," said Quillon.

"That close," said Stephanus, taking the tablet back. "Then we need to get you across that open field. That means we need a distraction."

Stephanus grabbed his handheld and said, "Willis, I want you to follow me. We'll each take up a position on the road, near the grocery store and the school. I want your squad to do a quick search of those buildings. We can't pull anyone out, but I want to know what we are dealing with. Miller, take up a position on the forest side. When we are ready, I want you to attack the creature to give us a distraction so I can get Quillon closer to the creature. That will probably be the merry-go-round near the swings. If the creature runs, I want Miller to follow and attack as opportunities present themselves."

Quillon sat up straight as they entered the village. There were signs of damage caused by the creature as it traveled down the Main Street towards its current resting place. He could see damage to walls and a few enlarged windows, as if something punched its way through them. There was no one in sight. But there were a few signs of victims, from blood stains to debris of bodies quickly picked over then dropped for the next tender morsel. A general evacuation order had been given, but it was obvious not everyone had made it out.

"Focus on what's next," said Stephanus. "I've been told you cannot move under your own power once you have linked with the creature. Is that true?"

"Yes," said Quillon, remembering back to his vision of him in the library and the control room. "I also have had trouble breaking off my link."

"Understood," said Stephanus. "We'll figure out how to deal with that when the time comes. Get ready, We're here."

Quillon felt the vehicle swerve, then come to a quick halt. He recognized the grocery store from the video and could see the playground, but the building still blocked the view of the creature. The other vehicle continued past them and stopped near the neighboring building, the school. Tetherball poles and hopscotch areas and a few small benches filled the sizable gap between them.

The security officers, all armed with automatic weapons, quickly jumped out of their vehicles. One from each vehicle headed toward the nearest building entrances, first aid kit in hand.

"Do what you can, but remember, we are here for the creature. Leave the bag if needed and get back here," Stephanus looked back at Quillon who was still sitting in the vehicle. Looking at the open playground. "Out now!"

Quillon blinked, then moved toward the door. Once outside, he could smell the faint traces of something burning. Except for the sounds of the men nearby, it was quiet. No birds, no screaming, Nothing. A terrifying sound soon interrupted that silence. "It knows I'm here!" he said.

"Stay with me," said Stephanus as he walked to the back of the SUV and opened the back.

When Quillon joined him, Stephanus had the trunk panel up and was looking over a collection of weapons, which included two rocket-propelled grenade launchers.

Stephanus grabbed an automatic rifle and ammunition. As he was closing the lid, he said, "My private collection." He headed for the front of the vehicle and said, "Can you link from here?"

Quillon said, "Yes, but if I move the portal, it is going to end up near here."

"Okay. Then we need to get you closer. How much time do you need?"

"Maybe five minutes," said Quillon with a shrug. "It works better if I'm under pressure."

"That won't be a problem," said Stephanus. "Willis, Jamison, what's the story?" he asked into his radio.

"No one is alive in the grocery store." Came the response from Willis. "We have about ten kids and two adults in here," said Jamison. "One adult is badly wounded."

"Give them the med kit, tell them not to move. I need both of you back here," said Stephanus. He paused for a second, then said, "Miller, you in position?"

"We are setup but if it moves, it could leave our line of sight."

"Okay, we are going to take up a position at the little merry-go-round," said Stephanus. "When we do, I need you to open up on it. Keep hitting it while Quillon does his thing."

When Willis and Jamison returned, Stephanus pointed at them and said, "You two, with me." He looked at the others and said, "Cover our retreat if needed, but make sure we are out of the way first."

Quillon looked at the distance to the merry-go-round and his knees shook.

"Okay Miller, light it up," said Stephanus.

The sound of gunfire and the screaming from the creature were almost enough to cause Quillon to run. Before he could, Stephanus dragged him toward the screaming creature.

He was at the merry-go-round before he could take a breath. Stephanus pushed him to the ground and shouted, "Do it!"

Quillon looked up at the creature and could only stare, openmouthed. It looked big while it was sleeping in the drone video, but now it looked gigantic. The creature's body was raised up with its shell turned toward the oncoming bullets. Its tentacles swinging and smashing in every direction.

Stephanus gave Quillon a slap on the back of his head and shouted, "Do it now! I'm warning you, if we need to run, I'm leaving you here."

Quillon nodded and, laying on his back, covered his ears and forced himself to think about the box and dagger. Suddenly, he sat up and said, "The box. I forgot it in the car. I need it for this to work."

Stephanus clinched his fist and stared at Quillon like he was going to strike him. He looked at the others with him and said, "I'll be right back. Give him cover if needed," then he was off running for the SUV.

"The bullets aren't doing anything. Its shell is too hard," said Willis.

"You better know what you're doing because I will not die for you!" said Jamison.

Seconds later, the sound of gunfire stopped, but the creature's screaming didn't. It got louder and seemed closer. Quillon looked in the creature's direction and saw it rapidly heading his way. He could sense the anger as he watched the tentacles raise up. They hovered in the air long enough for Quillon to roll away a few times before they came crashing down on the merry-go-round. The screaming of the creature was joined by the two men just a few feet from him. Quillon looked back in time to see Jamison being crushed under the weight of a huge tentacle. Flying metal from the merry-go-round had struck Willis. He was attempting to crawl away when several tentacles fought over him, with the victor dragging him screaming toward the gaping mouth of the creature.

Quillon grabbed a nearby rifle, pointed it at the creature, and fired. The creature dropped Willis and stared at Quillon. He could see in its eyes it recognized him.

It roared a sound that almost sounded like laugh, as Quillon did his best to slide himself backwards.

The flash of fire and an explosion left both Quillon and the creature stunned. Someone grabbed him from behind, shoved the box in his hands and said, "Get Busy!" It was then that Quillon understood Stephanus had used some of his private stock to save him.

Quillon opened the box and held the dagger in his hand. The connection to the portal came with a trickle of pain in his chest. He closed his eyes and imagined the portal sitting beside the creature. The pop, followed by a sucking sound and the familiar stench, told him it had worked. He opened his eyes and stared in misbelief.

"What happened to it?" asked Stephanus. "What did you do wrong?"

The portal was there, floating in air, right where Quillon wanted it, but it was smaller, too small for the creature to pass through.

"We need blood," said Quillon. "The dagger needs blood for the portal to grow." Quillon looked at the mangled body of Jamison near him, took the dagger, and plunged it into it. He could see and feel the response from the portal as it increased in size.

"The creature is going to wake up before that thing gets to full size." said Stephanus, picking up a rifle from the ground. "Let's go. You can link with it in the car."

"Okay," said Quillon, but as he got up, he could feel the creature stirring. "No time. I got to link now," he said, closing his eyes and holding the box close to his chest. Soon, his mind flooded with feelings of pain and anger.

Opening his eyes, he saw himself sitting with the box against his chest. He felt the urge to reach out and crush both himself and the box. Quillon forced the creature to look at the portal. He could see the size slowly growing and felt the start of the tug from it. A chill ran through his body, and he knew the creature was afraid. It had forgotten about Quillon and the box and now only wanted to get away from the tug of the portal.

Knowing the creatures' attention would soon return to his helpless body, Quillon struggled to control its movements, fighting to move it toward the portal. He needed help and called out to Henrietta as he had done in the past.

The tingle of the tattoo let Quillon know she was there. His relief quickly vanished when he saw her stepping toward the creature and his body slowly advancing, like a zombie, toward the creature behind her. He wanted to yell for Henrietta to stop, but all that came out was the horrible sound of the creature.

Seeing himself blindly walking between tentacles caused a momentary loss of control. He struggled to get it back, but no matter how hard he tried, he couldn't prevent one of the smaller tentacles from wrapping around his leg. He watched helplessly as it dragged his body towards the creature.

He didn't feel the pain but knew it was there and yelled anyway. He felt anger and put that feeling to work, trying to force the creature to release his leg. Just as he was being lifted by his leg from the ground, there was another explosion.

When Quillon opened his eyes, he found himself back in his body, lying on the ground. His ears were ringing, his leg hurt, and his shoulder ached from where it hit the ground. A few feet from him lay the creature. It wasn't moving, but he could see it was still alive. Looking back, he saw Stephanus lower his RPG launcher and say, "That's all I got. Do something now!"

Quillon looked at Henrietta, who was standing by the portal. He knew this was his only chance to move the creature into the portal. The link came much easier with almost no resistance. *It's stunned again. I only hope I can make it move,* he thought.

It felt like he was carrying a tremendous weight. His feet moved like he was walking through thick mud. It took all his effort to move it towards the portal. The closer he got, the stronger the pull from the portal. Soon that pull was helping him advance until Quillon felt himself stumble through the portal threshold. Looking around, a feeling of relief came over him and he was actually glad to be back in this alien place.

Looking back through the portal, he saw Henrietta standing by his body. She beckoned him. *I almost forgot,* he thought. He knew he needed to act fast. The portal was still open, and he could feel the creature's mind stir.

As Quillon released his link with the creature, his first thought was for the dagger. His leg hurt and he almost crawled to Jamison's body. Pulling the dagger loose, he looked for the box and saw it a few feet from where he had just been, laying there at Henrietta's feet. The pain in his leg was increasing and the roar of the creature told him time was almost up. *It's too far,* he thought. In desperation, he yelled for Henrietta to bring it, because he could think of nothing else.

A hand grabbed him by his arm and dragged him towards the box. As he rolled on to his back he saw Stephanus, eyes fixed on the portal, rifle in his free hand. He heaved Quillon toward the box and said, "I was told if you can't close that thing, your death might close it. Get busy. If I see that thing coming out, you're dead!"

Quillon watch as Stephanus ran for the SUV. The threat left him in a state of panic, not sure who would kill him first.

The roar of the creature forced him from his daze. He opened the box, shoved the dagger inside, and rolled on his side so he could see the portal. It was still wide open. Nothing happened.

Quillon glanced back toward Stephanus, but couldn't see him. His hands trembled. The creature let out another roar and he could see tentacles start tentatively to reach through the portal.

Quillon rolled on his stomach, putting all his weight on the box, hoping it would close. "No!" He shouted. "This is not how it happened in the dream. Why did you show me that if it wouldn't work?"

Emotion overwhelmed him, and he could not hold back the tears. Between his sobs and the cry from the creature, he felt warming on his back. He held his breath, as he was sure someone was touching him. Soon the burning spread to his whole back. He stopped crying and screamed with pain, which was mixed with the scream from the creature, the roar of the portal, and the sound of gunfire. There was a loud sucking sound, then a pop, leaving only his cries of pain, which thankfully soon ended.

Quillon rolled on his side and saw that the portal was gone. On the ground, below where it had been, he saw several wiggling tentacles severed by the closing portal. He sat up slowly, held the box out before him, and let out a sigh when he saw it was closed.

Feeling a hand on his shoulder, Quillon turned, expecting to see Stephanus, but found Henrietta standing there. "Thank you, Henrietta," he said, reaching out for her but only finding air.

Quillon glanced at his hand, confused. He knew she had touched him. When he looked back, the image of his beloved little sister blurred, and slowly changed back into the blond hair girl he had seen sacrificed in his dream. "Where is Henrietta?" He asked. The girl smiled and then vanished.

Chapter 30
Your Choice

Quillon sat, as best he could, rubbing his injured legged. He stared at the spot where Henrietta had been, playing the memory of her change repeatedly in his head. The last few times he had seen Henrietta, he almost felt that she needed him, like she had finally forgiven him for what happened. When she changed into someone else, it scared him. He worried that someone or something had been playing with him. Quillon closed his eyes, seeing Henrietta in his mind. When he opened his eyes, she was still gone. "I don't understand, Henrietta," he said, hoping she would appear again and explain what he had seen.

Looking at the box in his lap, he was relieved to see that the pattern was no longer moving, and the box appeared finally to be closed for good. At least he could be sure of one thing.

He watched as the security did their best to clean up the mess the creature had left. He stared at the scar the portal had left on the playground grass, just feet away, wondering if that or this village would ever return to normal.

Stephanus had stopped by earlier to make sure he was okay. He took the Necro Box from Quillon and said, "Someone will come for you. Don't make me go looking for you." With that, Quillon was alone.

He looked up, closed his eyes, and took a deep breath. The sun on his face felt good, and he felt a sense of relief even if the air still had the stench of the portal and the light smell of smoke. "It's over, now I can go home." he said, not caring if anyone heard him.

The sound of buzzing interrupted his moment of comfort, like that of a persistent fly. *Dead bodies,* he thought, as the vision of remains of the people killed by the creature came to his mind. When the sound got louder, he knew what it was. Looking around, he saw a pair of drones above him. He smiled and thought, *I'm going to check that video out when I get back.* A few seconds later, he laughed. "Get back," he said. "I'm talking like I want to go back to that place."

Quillon looked at the town, just a few dozen yards ahead, and thought about his chances of running. He wondered if anyone from outside the Foundation would show up to help. Someone that could help him. Someone he could tell his story to.

Behind him, he heard a vehicle and knew his chance had passed. Quillon glanced over his shoulder and saw a single SUV. It surprised him when Yuri got out. He had expected Georges.

Quillon looked back up at the drones and then toward the ruins of the town. Seeing Yuri now brought back his talk about the zoo. "Endangered Species," he mumbled.

He heard the footsteps stop behind him and knew it was time to go. Standing up, Quillon turned slowly to face Yuri, who said nothing, but looked around at the aftermath.

"What now?" asked Quillon. "Back to the Zoo?"

"You were listening," said Yuri, still looking around. "That's good." He put his hand on Quillon's shoulder for a second, then said, "Walk with me."

Quillon stared at Yuri as he headed toward where the portal had been. His leg hurt and he was tired and really didn't want to do anything but rest. When Yuri stopped and looked back at him, Quillon sighed and limped toward him.

"You're hurt." Yuri paused, then with a smile said, "I will make sure that gets taken care of."

"Thank you," said Quillon, rubbing his knee. "I was expecting Professor Georges."

Yuri turned to face Quillon, looked around, then said, "The Regents offered him a retirement opportunity, and they asked me to take his place." He smiled again and said, "Even though you closed the portal, ending this incident, they could not forgive him for putting the Foundation at such risk of discovery."

"Retirement. What does that mean?" asked Quillon.

Yuri looked over the top of his chrome sunglasses and said, "I think it would be wiser for you to ask what's next for you."

Quillon felt a chill run up his back. That definitely sounded like a threat. He studied Yuri, wishing he would take off his glasses so he could see his eyes. He did not know how to answer Yuri, so he didn't.

"I see I have your attention. Good," said Yuri. "The other Regents, and I had a long talk while you were out here risking your life for us. We decided it would be only fair to give you a choice about your future."

"I want to go home," said Quillon as soon as Yuri finished. "They promised me that if I closed the portal, I could go home."

"I think you should listen to the choices before you answer," said Yuri. The tone of his voice became more serious, and he continued, "I will say that each comes with what could be unpleasant conditions."

Before Quillon could say anything, Stephanus joined them. "It's going to take us some time before we finish here."

"How bad?" asked Yuri.

"I lost two men, and it looks like it killed about twelve people in the village. We have another eight injured. I will know better once we do a roster check. Plus, we still need to make sure no videos or messages leaked out."

"Good Job. Keep me informed," said Yuri. "Oh, and there will be some staff changes for you to deal with once you're done."

"Really?" said Stephanus, looking at Quillon.

"I'm sure your office has notified you of the major ones."

"Yes, Grand Master," said Stephanus. "And the current matter?"

"Quillon and I were just discussing that. I will let you know the outcome soon."

"Thank you, sir," said Stephanus,

The look Stephanus gave him before walking off truly scared Quillon. "Look, I don't know what you have planned for me, but I don't want to die," said Quillon, stepping a few steps back from Yuri, his hands before him defensively.

"I'm glad to hear that," said Yuri. "It was the choice I hoped you would make."

Quillon relaxed slightly and asked, "Does that mean I can go home now?"

"Unfortunately, no," said Yuri. "What it means is you can read about your funeral instead of being a part of it."

"My funeral?" said Quillon, not sure he understood him.

"You possess a valuable commodity," said Yuri, looking around again. "Besides the fragments in your chest. You can open and close the box, not to mention link with the creature held in the portal. It has become clear that someone on the inside has been sharing information about the box and we can only assume about you as well. That means Quillon Thomas needs to die and the box and all its forbidden knowledge must disappear as well."

"Die? You just said I could live."

"You can, but your namesake and the life it leads can't," said Yuri.

Quillon was quiet for several minutes.

Yuri waited patiently, then said, "You said you remembered my talk about the zoo." When Quillon nodded, Yuri continued, "Think of me as your caretaker, and I can promise you a very nice cage. But I need to make one thing clear. Even though it won't look like a cage, if you try to escape, or someone comes looking for you, we will have no choice but to put you in that empty coffin."

Quillon did not know what to say. He believed Yuri's threat and just nodded his understanding.

"Good," said Yuri as he put his hand on Quillon's shoulder and gently guided him back toward Yuri's car. "Just so you know. We are not going back to the Foundation. My people are going to take you some place and introduce you to the new you. It may not seem like it now, but believe me, you made the right choice."

As Quillon walked toward the SUV, he thought about the people he would leave behind. He would miss his parents, even though they had stopped talking to each other long ago. He would also miss Glenn, the one person who had stuck with him during his treatment. Quillon even realized he would miss his therapist, who had spent years convincing him to ignore Henrietta's request to join her.

Quillon stopped and glanced to where he had last seen Henrietta. He had only wanted to make things right with her. Quillon wasn't sure what happened with Henrietta in the end, but it looked like she was going to get her wish.

That thought cheered him a bit as he limped toward the waiting SUV and the life of a stranger.

Author's Note

When I started this book, I created a planning document that described the basic story concept. It also included my thoughts about an ending.

As I wrote the book, I found the story suggesting another ending. I followed its prompting and felt good about the results. This darker ending didn't get the reception I expected, so I went back to the drawing board.

I struggled with creating another ending, but finally arrived at the current one. It required that I go back into the story and drop in details to support it. Yuri's talk about the Zoo was one of those items.

Now that it's done, I'm not sure which ending is better, so I have included both.

Feel free to let me know which you like. My email address is in the front of the book.

Alternate Ending

Quillon sat as best he could, rubbing his injured legged. He stared at the spot where Henrietta had been, playing the memory of her change repeatedly in his head. The last few times he had seen Henrietta, he almost felt that she needed him, like she had finally forgiven him for what happened. When she changed into someone else, it scared him. He worried that someone or something had been playing with him. Quillon closed his eyes, seeing Henrietta in his mind. When he opened his eyes, she was still gone. "I don't understand, Henrietta," he said, hoping she would appear again and explain what he had seen.

Looking at the box in his lap, he was relieved to see that the pattern was no longer moving, and the box appeared finally to be closed for good. At least he could be sure of one thing.

He watched as the security did their best to clean up the mess the creature had left. He stared at the scar the portal had left on the playground grass, just feet away, wondering if that or this village would ever return to normal.

Stephanus had stopped by earlier to make sure he was okay. He said, "Someone will come for you. Don't make me go looking for you." With that, Quillon was alone.

He looked up, closed his eyes, and took a deep breath. The sun on his face felt good, and he felt a sense of relief even if the air still had the stench of the portal and the light smell of smoke. "It's over, now I can go home." he said, not caring if anyone heard him.

The sound of buzzing interrupted his moment of comfort, like that of a persistent fly. *Dead bodies,* he thought, as the vision of remains of the people killed by the creature came to his mind. When the sound got louder, he knew what it was. Looking around, he saw a pair of drones above him. He smiled and thought, *I'm going to check that video out when I get back.* A few seconds later, he laughed. "Get back," he said. "I'm talking like I want to go back to that place."

Quillon looked at the town, just a few dozen yards ahead, and thought about his chances of running. He wondered if anyone from outside the Foundation would show up to help. Someone that could help him. Someone he could tell his story to.

Behind him, he heard a vehicle and knew his chance had passed. Quillon glanced over his shoulder and saw a single SUV. He watched as Georges stepped out, followed by security.

Quillon looked back up at the drones and then toward the ruins of the town and took in what little peace he could before they would force him back into the madness of the Foundation.

He heard the footsteps stop behind him and knew it was time to go. Standing up, Quillon turned slowly to face Georges, who was just a few feet away. He did not see the congratulatory expression he had hoped for. Quillon extended the box toward Georges and was startled to see that the hand that reached back was holding a gun. The sound of the gun going off surprised him more than the pain of the bullet entering his chest. Quillon pulled his hands back, clasping the box to his chest as if to stop the pain. He dropped to his knees before falling to the ground in a fetal position.

Quillon felt his heart beating, and there was a ringing in his ears. His chest ached, and his breathing struggled. He looked up at Georges, gun still in his hand. He couldn't find the breath to ask why.

Georges handed the gun to a nearby guard. Then, as if understanding the question that Quillon was trying to ask, said, "I'm sorry Quillon. I really am, but there was no other choice. The creature is gone now, but that leaves us with you, the only person who can open and close the box. We tried to think of some way to save you, but everyone agreed you are too dangerous."

Georges reached for the box, but Quillon held it tight to his chest with what little strength he had left.

"Quillon, let go or I am going to have this man shoot you in the face," said Georges.

Quillon could feel his strength leaving as the box, now covered with the blood from his chest, fell from his grip.

Georges reached down to retrieve the box and watched as the dagger fell from it, almost in slow motion, landing in the pool of blood flowing from Quillon's chest.

Quillon looked back up at Georges just as the pain in his chest took his breath away. Then, as his vision dimmed, he heard the pop and sucking sound behind him, followed by a terrifying roar. The last thing Quillon saw was the look of terror in Georges' eyes.

About the Author

Thank you for reading my book.

I am new to writing, but I'm hooked.

I truly enjoy planning and struggling through the development of a story. I feel like I am on a great adventure, one I hope I can successfully share with my readers.

I do believe writing is a shared adventure, and I welcome your comments and suggestions.

Read more at https://www.facebook.com/JCrosbybooks/.

CPSIA information can be obtained
at www.ICGtesting.com
Printed in the USA
JSHW081931160523
41775JS00001B/97

9 781735 938752